About the Author

A person of many interests, Holly Franklin has worked as a social worker, an antiques dealer, an editor, a personal chef, a dog boarding kennel owner and a financial services rep. She has four grown children, four grandchildren, two dogs and one marvelous husband. *loosecannon* is her first novel, and she is now working on a book of dog stories.

loosecannon is a work of fiction. The author has taken great liberties with places, names, etc., with respect to the City of Guelph. Her account of the beginning of the Italian Canadian Club is also fictitious in order to benefit the characters in *loosecannon*. As with many other writers, she may begin with a real event or person, but very quickly the event or person takes on a life of its own so that she merely follows it to wherever it is headed. And she is often amazed at the end result.

loosecannon

Holly Franklin

loosecannon

Olympia Publishers
London

www.olympiapublishers.com
OLYMPIA PAPERBACK EDITION

Copyright © Holly Franklin 2024

The right of Holly Franklin to be identified as author of
this work has been asserted in accordance with sections 77 and 78 of
the Copyright, Designs and Patents Act 1988.

All Rights Reserved

No reproduction, copy or transmission of this publication
may be made without written permission.
No paragraph of this publication may be reproduced,
copied or transmitted save with the written permission of the publisher,
or in accordance with the provisions
of the Copyright Act 1956 (as amended).

Any person who commits any unauthorized act in relation to
this publication may be liable to criminal
prosecution and civil claims for damage.

A CIP catalogue record for this title is
available from the British Library.

ISBN: 978-1-80439-285-0

This is a work of fiction.
Names, characters, places and incidents originate from the writer's
imagination. Any resemblance to actual persons, living or dead, is
purely coincidental.

First Published in 2024

Olympia Publishers
Tallis House
2 Tallis Street
London
EC4Y 0AB

Printed in Great Britain

Dedication

My husband, Casey, has been more than supportive and encouraging while I have written *loosecannon*. On a daily basis I try to live up to his esteem and love for me. I only hope that his confidence is not misplaced!

Acknowledgements

Although no one has read the entire manuscript, I am blessed by the encouragement of my two best friends, Dr. Douglas Reberg and Anne Davis Latham. Thank you both for a life-time of love and support.

Very unfortunately, Doug died this past summer, in Stratford, Ontario. His death, precipitously swift, has stunned those of us who knew and loved him, none more so than me and my four sons. He was brilliant, erudite and thigh-slapping funny, not necessarily in that order. He was also the most generous and loving person I've ever had the honor of knowing. Always in our thoughts and hearts, Doctor Doug.

    Dr. Douglas Charles Reberg, November 17, 1942 - August 12, 2023.

Chapter 1

"Toni, it's Viv."

"Viv. I've been meaning to call. How are you?" She leaned back from her desk, tucking the phone between her chin and shoulder. Her friend Viv would provide a much-needed respite from keying case notes into the computer.

"I don't know where to start..." Her voice quavered on the last word.

Toni sat up suddenly, her need for relief gone. "Talk to me, Viv. What's happening?"

"It's Bruce. He's driving me crazy. I'm afraid there's something wrong with him, and I don't have a clue what it's about. Last night we had dinner together and I'm afraid we had a bit too much to drink. He started saying and doing things that were nutty. I'm really worried about him." Toni heard her friend blow her nose.

"What kinds of things, Viv?" Her hand tightened around the receiver.

"After we separated last summer, I began seeing a man named Max, as you know. Bruce seemed okay with it. Our separation had been a mutual decision, and we agreed that we would be free to date other people. Lately, however, I have the feeling that Bruce has been following me. And last night, while we were drinking, Bruce phoned Max and told him that his (Bruce's) mental problems were over, and that Max could phone me whenever he wanted to. Max called me this morning and asked what that phone call was about. He was as confused about this as I am."

"Oh, honey. What else?"

"It gets worse. He told me that he'd had an affair with his cousin, Cynthia. I freaked, to put it mildly."

"My God." As a therapist, Toni thought she'd heard it all, but this disturbing revelation was about her colleague. Toni left her chair and started to pace. "What can I do to help, Viv?"

"I-I don't know." Tears returned to her voice. "Do you guys still meet for supervision? Maybe you could find some excuse to talk to him, try and find out what's bothering him? I'm at a loss."

Toni gazed out her office window, not seeing the blaze of colors on the old maples that lined Woolwich Street on this warm autumn day. She shivered, pulling her jacket together in an attempt to find some measure of psychic comfort.

Her friend caught her hesitation, interpreted it incorrectly. "Forget about it, Toni – I'm asking too much of you. I shouldn't be putting you in the middle of our mess – you've been a good friend to both of us, and I'm not being fair."

"I meant it, Viv – I want to help. I'll give you a call tomorrow. Get back to work and I'll see what I can do."

"Thanks so much, Toni."

Toni sank back into her chair and ran her hand through her hair. She thought back to her last conversation with Bruce. He'd seemed brittle, distracted.

She had gone up to his office for a case consultation, at his request. Their formal supervision days were over, but Bruce still relied on Toni for occasional help with difficult clients.

Bruce's smile when he said hello didn't reach his eyes. He lifted his cup of coffee and his hand shook. They discussed his case briefly.

"How are you doing, Bruce?" She tried to keep the concern out of her voice. He really didn't look good. She'd noticed a box of books on the floor beside his desk. Bruce's hand-writing was on the side of the box. She turned slightly in her chair to read what he'd written: "Bruce's books – who cares?" Oh, dear. His personal problems seemed to be invading his professional life.

"Okay, I guess." He didn't look up, and his voice held a measure of self-pity that Toni knew would take hours to unravel. She didn't think she was up to it right then. She reached across his desk and patted his hand as she rose from her seat.

"Call me later if you want to talk. I'll be at the university this afternoon, then home." She knew that if she postponed his desire to spill forth his problems, chances were good that time would solve some of them. She hoped.

Now she wondered if his personality disorder was getting worse. As a therapist, she realized how difficult it was to deal with borderline personalities. They were like bottomless pits. No matter how much or often you attempted to help, it was never enough. They latched onto people like blood-suckers in a murky pond. Most therapists ran the other way rather than attempt treatment. A fellow therapist had put his avoidance of borderlines succinctly, "Give me a garden-variety neurotic any day."

Nothing for it but to do it, Toni, she admonished herself now. She saved her notes and closed down the computer, gathered up her briefcase, and turned off the office lights, locking the door behind her. As she stepped into the vestibule of the century-old building, she noticed the light still on at the receptionist's desk. Roxie, her shining blonde hair bent over a romance novel, looked up guiltily when she saw Toni watching her. She greeted Toni as she slipped the Harlequin beneath her desk.

"Hi, Ms. Rossi…"

"Roxie – you make me feel like my mom. Please call me Toni, okay?"

"Okay, Toni," she said with reluctance.

"Is Bruce still up in his office by any chance?"

"He never came back from lunch, Ms.... I mean, Toni."

Toni felt a small frisson of guilty relief sweep over her. "Thanks, Roxie. I'll catch him tomorrow, then. Goodnight."

"Night, Toni."

She pushed open one side of the beautiful old etched-glass front door and turned the corner onto McTague Street. She'd left her car at home today, not needing to use it for an out-of-office appointment. She loved the four-block walk between her house and work. Both her home and office were in one of the oldest areas of Guelph, and she always felt fortunate to live and work in such a beautiful area. When she reached Exhibition Park, she turned toward London Road and walked down the slight incline to Glasgow Street. Turning onto Glasgow, she could see the lights upstairs in Hank's apartment. The knowledge that he was home caused her soul to stir in spite of herself. Stop it, she warned her errant thoughts. As if she had any control in that area.

She walked down the short side driveway to her apartment's entrance on the ground floor. When she opened her door, she was greeted by a large ginger-and-white tabby cat, who proceeded to wind himself around her legs, purring loudly. She reached down to stroke his head. "Hey, Humphrey."

At that same instant, she became aware that someone was sitting in the rocker in the dim corner of her kitchen, watching her.

"Hello, Antonia," the voice said, as cold as ever. "Long time no see."

Chapter 2

"Get out of here, James," Toni ordered. She thrust the back door open. "Right now."

James leaned back in the rocking chair. He rocked back and forth a few times before responding. "Relax, Toni. I just came here to talk to you."

She moved toward the phone, keeping her eyes on James. "Leave or I will call the police."

James stopped rocking. "You're not being very friendly, sweetheart. I thought that for old time's sake, since I came so far just to talk to you…"

Toni suddenly thought that she could use this opportunity to find out a few details about her ex-husband. If she could stay cool enough so that he wouldn't catch on. "James," she began again, injecting a smile into her voice, "you surprised me by appearing like that, inside my apartment…"

"Surprisingly easy, my dear." His smile didn't reach his eyes that looked weary to the point of exhaustion. James had been a private investigator for a brief period before university. During their marriage, he had confided some of the sordid details about his cases, mostly fuel for divorce actions. He'd also regaled his young wife with tales of his lock-picking abilities.

Now she kept her face impassive, pretending to pick up cat fluff from the floor, moving closer to the door.

"You were never this nervous when we were married," James said.

Toni leaned against the doorframe, trying to appear less frazzled. "So, leave me your number and I'll call you when I'm a little more relaxed."

"I'll find you when the time comes, honey. You really lost your cool just now, even if you haven't lost your looks." His eyes traveled from her face to her breasts, slowly, as though he were a judge in a beauty contest.

Toni lost it. "Get out of here, you pig…" She was shrieking.

"Or what, you'll phone for help, from the doorway?" He leaned forward, seeming ready to spring from the rocker to prevent her from phoning or bolting out the door. "Control yourself, Toni. I really do not mean any harm."

"What you are doing is called harassment, James. I want you out of here."

"We were married, Toni. And now you treat me like this?" His voice held a boyish type of plea. It was a trick she remembered all too well from their years together.

"I thought we were married, too. And then…"

"Wasn't it punishment enough that I was forced to take a teaching job in Athabasca, northern Alberta, for God's sake, because no one would hire me anywhere else? And after three years, I still can't get tenure, even there." He sank back in the rocker, wiping his eyes with his hand.

"Your decision, James. It was completely up to you."

He straightened himself once more. "I need something, Antonia. My baby pictures. Mom gave them to you, didn't she? I want them back." His voice contained a whiny note she'd not heard in their years of marriage. He'd always been so confident, even when it appeared that he wouldn't succeed in achieving one of his goals. He was very competitive, viewed every "no" as a red flag, and never gave up. Even in her agitation, Toni saw that he didn't look well. His normally ruddy complexion was sallow; bruised shadows lay under his eyes.

Maybe Athabasca was taking its toll.

"Give me your address and I'll mail them to you," she said.

"No, no address."

He rose out of the chair and grabbed her arm. "Where are they? In there?"

He pulled her toward her small home office.

"James, relax, I'll get them for you. Just let go of my arm." He didn't loosen his grip, and she pretended it didn't hurt, patting his hand with her free one, trying to reassure him. She led him to the ochre-colored dry sink and pulled at the small drawer. The drawer stuck, and as Toni yanked at it, a tall glass vase teetered from its spot over the cutlery drawer and smashed to the floor. Water, flowers and shards of glass lay everywhere on the hardwood.

"Toni?" a voice called from the second floor, alarm shading its edges, followed by the sound of someone running down the front stairs. "Are you all right?" The familiar deep voice was now outside her living room door, in the front hall of the old house.

Toni pulled at the drawer and it suddenly opened. "Those are the photos," James hissed, grabbing several pictures. He dropped her arm and ran toward the kitchen. "I'll be back," he said as he rushed out the back door.

Toni hurried to open the front hallway door. "Hank, Hank, thank God you heard me." Hank held her for a second then ran past her to the open back door. James was gone. Hank returned to Toni, taking her hands in his, assessing her for any damage.

"Are you okay?"

"I'm fine," said Toni. She squeezed Hank's large hands, meeting his concerned look with a smile. Even in her present state, she felt the powerful connection between them. Hank and James couldn't be more different physically or in their attitudes toward her. Hank's fading strawberry-blonde hair was clipped short, his head a mass of soft curls. James still wore his long dark hair parted in the middle, caught in a ponytail at the back of his neck. Hank's blue eyes were hooded, focused entirely on her. She couldn't remember James' eyes appearing other than sardonic, even when he had repeated their wedding vows.

Why was she so reluctant to accept what both she and Hank knew was inevitable? Hank's love and patience for her seemed limitless. He kept his distance, sensitive to her confusion, her skittishness, her occasional need to deny what she was feeling for him. What if she couldn't commit to those feelings? What if he ran out of patience? These thoughts terrified her. 'Not now, Antonia, stop thinking that way...' She heard that interior voice of reason.

"Who was that?" Hank's concern brought her back.

"James. My ex-husband." She tried to keep the small tremor out of her voice.

"I thought he was off in the wilds of Alberta, communing with blackflies and Sheridan. Penning the definitive erudite treatise on Restoration literature. The world breathlessly waiting."

She ignored the tilt toward sarcasm. "So did I. I'm not sure why he's here. He insisted on taking back some baby pictures his mother gave me. He could've done that by phone. The most upsetting part is that he somehow broke into the house before I got home. He wouldn't tell me how he did it."

"Let's take a look. I don't like the sound of this at all." Hank headed toward the basement stairs, Toni following. They checked all the windows and the basement door that led out to the backyard. Back upstairs, he checked doors and windows and the state-of-the-art alarm system he'd recently had installed.

"He seems to have bypassed everything. I'll get someone from ADT to have a look. Meanwhile, we need to make sure this doesn't happen again, sweetie."

Toni shivered with pleasure, in spite of herself, at the "we". "I'm out of vases, Hank. How about a well-timed scream?"

"I'm not always here, unfortunately." Hank was a famous children's book author. Although he wrote at home, he was always in demand for readings, lectures and book tours. He was right. His schedule was busy and often kept him away many times during the year.

Toni spotted her car keys on the hook by the back door. "What about my car's panic alarm?"

"Good. Even if I'm not here, it might scare him enough to get him to leave. You've also got my pager number. If you can reach a phone. Let me talk to the alarm guy tomorrow. Maybe he'll have some ideas."

Chapter 3

Earlier that afternoon, the bus had let James off at Woolwich and London Road, heading north in a cloud of exhaust. The fumes filled his chest and the coughing returned, causing him to bend at the waist, stopping his attempt to cross the street. Horns blared and he was forced to step back onto the curb until the light changed again.

'Shit,' he thought, 'great timing for another coughing fit, the third in the last hour or so.' He'd left his puffer in the bathroom this morning and had forgotten to bring a bottle of water with him. 'Let's get this over with,' he thought, hurrying across the street against the light, moving as quickly as he dared toward his destination.

He turned left onto Glasgow Street and spotted number 224 on the right side of the old street, a handsome example of Victorian yellow brick, two stories, numerous original windows, and a wraparound porch garnished with corbels and fretwork.

He knew that his ex-wife wouldn't be home yet but wasn't certain about any other occupants of the house. He'd take his chances.

Relying on long-ago expertise as a private investigator, he managed to discreetly disarm the alarm system so that only a pro might know what he'd done. He used his picks to easily open the basement door. Moving swiftly and silently through the basement, he gained entrance to the first-floor flat.

'Very nice,' he thought as he enviously admired Toni's

choice of furnishings, rugs, and artwork. 'You've certainly come up in the world, haven't you...' He remembered the untutored young student he'd first known, how he'd carefully introduced her to the finer things in life and convinced her that his view of the world was the correct one. How most of the rest of the world was largely unwashed, illiterate and incapable of attaining the level of intellectual aplomb that he knew was his domain, his due, the Machiavellian one percent that mattered.

His hand caressed the soft velvet of an armchair in the living room. His eyes followed the swag of a watered-silk curtain that graced one of the windows. The old oriental carpet muffled his footsteps as he headed toward the back of the house. An outraged screech stopped him from going any further.

'Christ.' He shuddered before he realized he'd made a noise. 'What the hell was that?' A large orange-and-white streak shot past him into a room off the living room, leaving him shaken. 'Get a grip, James,' he admonished himself. 'Must've been some sort of cat-like thing. She always did have a soft spot for those damned fur-balls.' He began to sneeze, and he could feel his eyes watering. 'Terrific. Whatever it is, I'm allergic to it, on top of everything else that's wrong.' He wiped his nose on the sleeve of his jacket.

He reached the kitchen and sank into an old rocking chair tucked into the corner next to a large window. He'd run out of energy for the moment, a common occurrence for him, lately. The late afternoon autumn light was fading quickly, and the kitchen was dimly restful. He put his head back and rested it on the back of the rocker. He felt his eyes close.

He was startled awake by the sound of the outside door handle turning. The kitchen was dark. He remained where he was, partially hidden in the corner of the room. He heard, rather than saw, someone enter the room and flick on the light switch while leaning down to pat the purring cat thing, whose name, apparently, was Humphrey. "Hello, Antonia. Long time no see..."

He saw her startled expression, the look of instant recognition turning to revulsion that she tried, unsuccessfully, to hide. "Get out of here, James," she ordered, moving toward the door, which she opened again. "Right now." She pointed out the door, her arm straight and the look on her lovely face angry, determined.

She looked, as always, beautiful, in a Botticelli-like manner – long dark curls that tumbled in unruly abandon past her shoulders, large, dark eyes, luscious full mouth, slender figure in a very tasteful jacket and tailored pants. He would love to ruin all that beauty, to cause her the very same pain he'd endured for many years. That would have to wait, for now.

He took his time answering, as usual, his arrogance still a weapon used to belittle, delay, control. "Relax, Toni. I just came here to talk to you."

Clearly exasperated, she threatened to call the police. "And how would you do that, sweetheart?" He gestured at the phone, which was on the other side of him, beyond Toni's reach.

He remembered why he had come to her. "I need those baby pictures of me that Mom gave you. I want them back."

"Give me your address and I'll mail them to you."

"No, no address, I want them now." He sprang from the chair and grabbed her arm. He pulled her into her small office, heading for a dry sink that seemed to serve as a desk. "Get them, Toni. Now."

She seemed to heed his distress and took a softer approach. "Okay, James, let go of my arm and I'll get them for you." She tugged on a drawer that was stuck. At the same time, a vase of flowers teetered above the drawer, smashing onto the floor with a loud crash. A mess everywhere.

A heartbeat later, a deep voice called from upstairs, "Toni?" The sound of footsteps running down the stairs then the same voice, just outside her living room door at the front of the house. "What's going on?" Concern edged with alarm.

James reached into the drawer, grabbed some photos, dropped her arm, and ran for the back door, clutching the photos. "I'll be back," he hissed as he ran out the door.

James hid behind an old maple tree, the large trunk of which allowed him to see inside one of the living room windows without being noticed by the house's inhabitants. He watched as a short, rather stocky man pulled Toni into his arms and stroked her hair, murmuring into its dark recesses.

'So that's how it is, my lovely… we shall see about that. Whoever he is, he will rue the day he ever laid eyes on you when I am finished with you,' he thought. James turned abruptly and walked away.

Chapter 4

After Hank left, Toni sank into the same rocker that James had used in her kitchen. She turned on the old-fashioned bridge lamp behind her, and Humphrey jumped into her lap, did a quick turn and settled into a circle, purring loudly as she absently stroked his head.

The phone on the small desk rang, interrupting her thoughts. No more bad news, please, she prayed. "Hello?" Wariness made her voice sound tentative.

"Antonia, you okay?" Her mother's musical voice, its old-country accent still audible after more than forty years in Canada, came through warm, concerned.

"Hi, Mama. Everything's fine. It's been a long day, and Humphrey and I just sat down before you called." She didn't want to burden her parents with news of James' sudden reappearance. They'd never liked him but had accepted the marriage while it lasted. Their relief at its dissolution was palpable.

Dignified and respectful of Toni's feelings, they never bad-mouthed James either before or after the divorce. She loved them for their forbearance and for everything else. She once asked why they didn't like him. Her mother's response, restrained as usual, spoke volumes. "Hard to watch someone you love being treated bad."

"You don't sound too good, *cara*. You work too hard. You need to enjoy life more, see your friends, eat good food, drink some *vino...*"

"Mama," Toni interrupted. "I am fine, really." Her mother's radar, fine-tuned to everything her daughter didn't say, was picking up her recent distress.

"All right, dear. You just don't sound too good. We worry. Your father wants to say hello, too, *bambina*. But before I put him on, I want to remind you about Giuliana's birthday party. On Saturday."

Toni's niece, a gorgeous little girl, who reminded everyone of Toni at the same age, was having her third birthday. Her aunt was totally smitten by her niece's huge blue eyes, long black ringlets, intelligence and ability to make everyone laugh.

"I wouldn't miss it for the world, Mama. I've already bought her something."

"I'll see you then." Her mom said goodbye.

"How's my *bella ragazza*?" Her father's voice boomed all the way from Grange Street. Toni sometimes thought he didn't need a phone. He was becoming increasingly hard of hearing, a result of decades in the construction industry. He assumed everyone else was deaf, as well.

Toni held the phone away from her ear. "Great, Daddy. How about you? Are you managing to keep busy?" Her dad had retired the year before, turning over Rossi Construction Ltd. to Toni's brother, Freddo. Fred, armed with an engineering degree, was busy changing and expanding the business, not always to their father's liking. Mr. Rossi tried not to interfere, but Toni knew it caused him distress when Fred did something his father would never have done in the old days. Like the huge casino job.

Her parents, immigrants from a village south of Naples, had come to Canada to make a better life for their family, and Giovanni Rossi had worked extremely hard to support his

25

growing family. He disapproved of gamblers ("They no work for their money, don't deserve") and especially casino owners ("Crooks, Toni, all crooks"). She knew that relinquishing control to his son was hard for her dad, even though he'd planned to do so for many years. Toni also knew that Fred and his wife, Laura, none was having marital problems that threatened to spill over into Fred's busy construction career. He'd asked his sister to not say anything to their parents, hoping to achieve a peaceful resolution without family involvement. She had agreed to keep his secret.

"She keeps me busy, you Mama. I run here, I run there. Always something." She could hear exasperation as well as a life-time of affection in his voice. Her parents were totally devoted to each other and to their family. Toni envied them, realizing how fortunate she was to grow up with so much love, concern and support. One of her goals in life had always been to try and emulate that life with someone of her own. She'd stumbled badly with James.

After saying goodbye to her dad, she fed Humphrey and heated some vegetable soup for herself. She thought back to her marriage with James and how unhappy she'd been. His arrogance and emotional abuse became worse as time went by. If he wasn't ridiculing her, he ignored her. When they attended faculty parties, he would disappear almost as soon as they got in the door. If she wanted to tell him something, or leave early, she would find him in a dark corner, in animated conversation with some extremely attractive woman. His "research" assistants at the university all looked like candidates for Hugh Hefner's bunny mansion. She once asked him why he made these choices, and his response was his arrogant best. "If all the applicants are equal, I obviously choose the most attractive ones. I wouldn't want to be surrounded by ugly people, would I?" Toni often wondered if any men ever applied. She supposed that none were "equal" to the bunnies.

Her landlord, Hank, on the other hand, appeared to be the opposite – a delightful combination of humility and self-confidence radiated from him, mixed in with other attributes such as honesty, reliability, and a wicked sense of humor. But his two most valuable traits, as far as Toni was concerned, were his passionate enthusiasm for those he loved and his drop-dead loyalty to the same.

She knew he'd been married before and that he was still good friends with his ex-wife, with whom he shared custody of Rachel, their fifteen-year-old daughter. He never talked about his marriage or why it failed, and rarely mentioned Aviva, his Israeli-born agronomist wife. Toni knew that they had dinner together occasionally but otherwise knew little else about their post-divorce relationship.

From the moment she had arrived on Hank's doorstep, "Wanted" ad in hand, to look at his apartment for rent, his interest in her had been clear and strong. She knew that if she were less damaged by her relationship with James, she could reward Hank's love and attention without hesitation. In fact, one night a few weeks ago, when her guard was down – a combination of a stressful week with clients and too many glasses of sauvignon blanc – his passion seemed like just what she needed. The next morning, however, her guard returned, armed and ready for battle.

Hank was understandably confused, hurt. "Is it something I did, lovey? I thought we were finally on the same cloud together. What happened?" He looked so upset, hair in disarray, sitting on the edge of her bed, about to put his jeans on and start his day.

"It has nothing to do with you, Hank. Please believe me. I'm just not ready for this, for you." You'd never know it by what happened all night long, she thought. No wonder he was confused. Her body had responded to him as if it had been on the brink of starvation. As if it could never get enough of him. "I loved everything we did, said, didn't need to say. I just need more time, more space to get myself together. I'm sorry, truly I am."

He gathered her in his arms as a large tear slid down her cheek and dropped into the field of hair on his chest. "Don't worry about it, lovey. If I ever meet the schmuck who did this to you, I'm sure I'll have a few words to say to him."

The thought of short, stocky Hank Epstein confronting tall, aristocratic James Barrington the Third made her giggle, in spite of herself.

"What's so funny, bubbeleh?" He brushed her long dark hair from her face and kissed away the tracks of her tears.

If only getting rid of the damage done by James were so easy. Her confidence in herself and her ability to trust and make good choices had been shattered by his treatment of her. As a therapist, of course, she knew that regaining what she'd lost would take time. Time and tentative steps with someone like Hank to guide her along. It was her bad luck that he was so ready and she was only beginning the long journey to health.

"Wait for me, Hank?" She looked up at him, her soul in her eyes, pleading with him to understand.

His hooded blue eyes looked down, equally as serious. "As long as it takes, my love."

Now the phone rang again, causing her to jump in her seat. Humphrey let out a screech and tore off her lap and across the room. "Toni?" A very distraught Viv was on the phone.

'God, what now?' thought Toni. "What's wrong, Viv?"

"Could you come? I'm afraid Bruce is going to kill himself."

Chapter 5

Toni's professional reflexes snapped into place.

"Okay, Viv? I'm right here." 'This was not going to happen,' thought Toni. 'Not Bruce. Not on her shift.' A suicide had happened once before, and it had taken a long time for her to find her way back to a normal way of life. However, she never lost the feeling that she somehow could've prevented what had happened to her client. She would carry that guilt with her to the end of her life.

"Viv? Is he there?"

"No, Toni, I don't know where… that's the problem… Toni, please…"

"Sit tight, Viv. Go to your fridge, take something nice and sweet out of the freezer and start eating." This advice was completely non-professional. This was her mother's solution to calamities of many kinds. But hey, it worked for Toni as well. "I'll be there in ten."

Toni sped along Glasgow Street as fast as she dared, onto Suffolk, and then Woolwich, skirting the business section of downtown Guelph. As she waited at the lights to turn onto Eramosa, she glanced at the time on her old Mustang's dashboard. 10.43 p.m. 'Lord, would this day ever be over?' Crossing over the Eramosa River, she saw the lights reflected on the water from houses that backed onto the river. The river appeared dark, tranquil, the houses warm and safe. 'Would this were so,' thought Toni, fretting about her friend.

She parked behind a red pickup in Viv's driveway on Metcalf. All the lights were on in the small bungalow. Toni walked into the kitchen and found Viv standing in the middle of the room, looking at a clean spoon and an unopened carton of Häagen-Dazs' Delectable Danish ice cream.

She barely registered Toni's presence. "Bruce made his will tonight. He forced me to be a witness. He even called some stranger in off the street to be the other witness. My God. 'Now,' Bruce had said. 'I want to look after it now. Done.'" Viv's eyes held pools of tears waiting to spill.

"Where has he gone, Viv?"

"He left after the will signing. 'That's that,' he said and left. In a taxi."

"What about the truck?" Toni asked. Bruce had spent something close to sixty thousand dollars on a state-of-the-art brick-red Ford 350 pickup. He had intended to pull their Fifth Wheel Camper with it. "I saw it in the driveway…"

The tears began to slide down Viv's face and drip onto her sweater. She worked hard to keep her mouth from trembling. "I found this after he left." She handed a small government document to Toni. It was a signed change of ownership on the truck's vehicle registration. "He gave his truck to me." Viv hid her face behind one hand and turned away from Toni, shoulders heaving with silent sobs.

Toni turned her around so that Viv was facing her and held her arms firmly. "Sweetie, Bruce is being too obvious. He wants attention, that's all." Toni hoped like hell this was true. "Cry, Viv, cry. Open your mouth and let it all out – wail!" Viv managed a few coughing sounds. Toni adopted some of her mother's stricter tones. "Viv – don't be a *Mangiacake*."

Viv stopped crying and smiled weakly. "M*angiacake*." Viv

laughed and then hiccupped. This was an old joke for them, because Viv really was a *Mangiacake* – an Austrian cake-eater from generations back. They sat at the kitchen table and Toni fed Viv small spoonful of ice cream, quickly. The hiccupping stopped.

Bruce had left at about seven tonight, Viv said. She thought he'd left the truck with her because he'd been drinking before he disappeared into the taxi. But when he'd not returned for it by ten, Viv had gone out to the truck with Bruce's spare key to see if it was locked. That was when she found the lumpy envelope with her name on it on the driver's seat. Inside were Bruce's set of keys and the registration documents.

"I came in and called his apartment, but there was no answer. And his message box is full, so I couldn't even leave a message."

Viv and Toni decided to drive to Bruce's apartment on Cardigan Street.

They took Toni's black Mustang. No one answered the buzzer in the lobby, so Viv used her keys that Bruce had given to her to enter the building and then his apartment. Something blocked the door, so they pushed it slowly into the hallway of the apartment. The distinctive smell of cat litter badly in need of cleaning hit them before they stepped inside. A meowing cat rubbed itself rapidly against their legs. When Viv flipped the light switch on, they saw a stack of flyers, newspapers and mail behind the door.

"Where's he been staying then, if not here?" Toni asked.

"I have no idea. He comes by my house most days, often around suppertime, but he doesn't stay there at night. At work?"

They listened to Bruce's messages, Toni jotting down numbers. Meanwhile, Viv fed the cat a pack of dry cat food she found on a shelf, refilled its water bowl, and cleaned out its litter box. The first phone message was from a playful female voice that identified itself as Sheila. She had called three times to confirm dates.

Bruce must have kept them, because Sheila called a fourth time. Her final message mentioned dinner at eight on Thursday evening. Tonight. The other messages were several increasingly annoyed calls from Bruce's mother at a local nursing home.

The coquettish Sheila had left a phone number.

Toni dialed the number but there was no answer. It was almost midnight, after all.

The next stop for Toni and Viv was Toni's office, but no one was there, either. They finally headed back to Glasgow Street, both exhausted. Toni poured large brandies for both of them. As they sipped their drinks, Viv filled Toni in on some of Bruce's other increasingly strange behaviors. The night that Viv and her lover, Max, had had their first date, Bruce drove to Max's ex-wife's house to tattle on Viv and Max. Diana's hopes of a reconciliation with Max were dashed, needless to say.

Max discovered Bruce's visit to his ex-wife when a neighbor phoned Max to ask why there had been a large red pickup in Diana's driveway overnight. Viv was appalled that Bruce would try to hurt innocent Diana, as well as herself and Max, with his jealousy. Much to Bruce's dismay, Diana continued to hope for Max's return, and Max and Viv continued seeing each other.

On a recent Saturday morning, Viv had returned to her house after her daily run. She did her cool-down stretches on her back stoop, noting Bruce's pickup in her driveway. As she entered the kitchen, she saw Bruce sitting at the table, reading a thick binder. He looked up when he saw her, his face full of anger. He waved the binder in the air and said, "There's no mention of me in here – just Max, Max, Max."

When Viv realized that he was holding her private journal, she felt something in her snap. She ran toward him and tried to grab the journal away, but Bruce held it up, just out of her reach. She told Toni that she pounded on his chest, screaming at him, and then collapsed onto the floor, sobbing. Bruce knelt behind her, his arms around her, crooning into her ear, "It's okay, baby, I won't let you hurt yourself." She yelled at him that she had no intention of hurting herself but that she would gladly murder him just then.

She told Toni that his growing neediness and invasion of her privacy were what drove them further apart. However, she still worried about him, especially at times like tonight. He had been seeing a therapist, but one day announced that he was "cured" and stopped going. He'd often told her he wanted to "walk around inside her head". Viv shivered as she told Toni this. He'd begun phoning her school several times a day to see if she was there. And she'd heard, through her own lawyer, that Bruce's lawyer had got so fed up with Bruce's daily phone calls and interference with the separation agreement and divorce that she had fired him as a client.

Toni tucked Viv into the day bed in her living room and collapsed into her own bed shortly after. Humphrey curled around her back, purring softly.

At eight o'clock the next morning, Toni phoned Roxie to let her know she'd be a bit late. She told Roxie that she was still trying to find Bruce. "But he's here," said Roxie, a puzzled sound in her voice. "I'll put you through." Toni handed the phone to Viv.

"Sugar!" Bruce's voice boomed over the phone so loudly that even Toni could hear it. "How ya doing? Like my present?"

Viv looked stunned. "Bruce, I tried to leave you a message

last night, but your box was full. And your apartment..." Toni shook her head, and Viv stopped herself from telling him about their visit last night.

"Sorry, sugar, I haven't been there in a while. But, hey, it's a new day, and I'm a new man. I'll attend to my work here, then – why don't I have any appointments today? Roxie?" Viv could hear him shuffling papers on his desk. "Well, whatever. Then I'll go home and start there. Hey, life is good, isn't it, Viv?" Bruce was so full of himself he barely heard Viv's next question.

"So, where'd you go for dinner last night, Bruce?" Viv asked slowly.

"We went to this fabulous place in Rockwood, La Vieille Auberge. Have you been there? So romantic, and, well, actually, Viv, I went with this amazing... friend."

"Okay, Bruce, enough." Viv threw down the phone. "And to think I was worried about that snake. He was with the 'amazing' Sheila all that time."

And he'd completely forgotten about his cat, Toni thought. How do you forget something like that?

The phone rang again. It was Roxie from the office. "There's a message for you, about tonight. Someone named James stopped by here to say he was sorry about yesterday, and that he wants to make it up to you. He'll meet you at The Other Brother's restaurant at seven tonight, 'with bells on'. Those were his words."

James? Toni wondered. At her office, too?

"Toni?" Roxie again. "He didn't leave a phone number." It didn't sound as though Roxie had been favorably impressed by James, to say the least. "Who is this guy, anyway?"

Chapter 6

Hank closed his laptop and turned off the light on his desk. There were no sounds from his tenant's apartment downstairs, but he lifted the shade to see if her car was in the driveway below, anyway. No sign of her car tucked in behind his. He felt a sense of disappointment. She was often out in the evening, either with work commitments or dinner with friends. He vowed not to worry about her, even though he found it difficult not to, after the events the other evening with her ex-husband. What kind of an idiot pulls a stunt like that, he wondered. A sneaky one, that's who. Neither the locksmith nor the alarm people could figure out how James had managed to bypass their safeguards. He hoped that was the last of Toni's ex-husband's subterfuges.

He wandered into the kitchen, opened his fridge and took out a beer. As he drank, he thought about meeting Toni and how things had changed since that day. He had posted the apartment for rent as soon as the previous tenants left. They were an older married couple off to Europe for an extended vacation in France, their return date unknown. They had insisted Hank rent out the flat downstairs to someone else. He was reluctant to do so, as they'd become friends, and he looked forward to seeing them on their return. However, they were indefinite about when or if they would be back in Guelph.

When he had answered the doorbell after a phone call from a prospective tenant, he was unprepared for the rush of feelings that engulfed him at the sight of Toni. She was drop-dead gorgeous but had the demeanor of a lost waif looking for a safe harbor. He knew that he said hello, shook her hand and invited her into the vestibule at the front of the house but was hard-pressed to remember what else was said. She had a musical voice that made him forget his manners and the reason why she was in his house. Recovering his bearings, he ushered her into the downstairs flat and began to show her the rooms. He tried to see them through her eyes but found it difficult to concentrate.

She asked him a question but had to repeat it before he understood what she was asking. "I have a cat – he's a rescue that I found at the Guelph Humane Society after my divorce. He's about three years old, a ginger tabby, house-trained, neutered and very friendly. Would you be okay with him in the flat? His name is Humphrey."

At this point, Hank had thought, I'd welcome a Bengal tiger into the flat if you asked, but replied, "Of course. I love animals. In fact, if I wasn't on book tours so often, I'd have at least one cat or dog myself." He tried to stop the silly grin he thought must be plastered on his face. 'Get a grip, Hank. She'll think you are an idiot.'

They had looked through the rest of the flat, viewed the furnace and utilities in the basement and left through the door into the backyard. "It's beautiful here," she said, looking up at him with a smile that lit up her face.

"It certainly is," Hank answered, basking in that smile.

And so Toni and Humphrey moved in with the help of her brother, Fred, and her work partner, Bruce. Both men were solicitous of Toni and treated her with respect and care, asking her advice about where to place the furniture and other household items instead of making assumptions about where to put her things. Fred was a large, handsome Italian-looking guy who clearly adored his sister; Bruce, on the other hand, struck Hank as an odd guy who treated everything as a joke. I wonder what he is covering up, Hank thought. I'll ask Toni about him when the moment is right.

When they had finished the move, Hank offered to get a beer for everyone, but both men declined and Toni tried to hide the exhaustion she was feeling. The men said their goodbyes to Hank, hugged Toni, and left. Toni released a very patient Humphrey from his crate; the cat proceeded to inspect every room and piece of furniture in the flat. Hank helped Toni set up a litterbox in the bathroom, and Toni fed and watered a ravenous kitty.

Hank left his cell number and his landline for Toni in case she had any questions and told Toni that if she needed anything to either call him or, better still, knock on the door in the front hallway that led up to his apartment. He was very inclined to linger in the flat with his new tenant but told himself to leave it be. Maybe a dinner or a drink would be appropriate in the near future. He certainly hoped so.

Chapter 7

When Toni thought of her older brother, Fred, she always remembered their childhood times with a smile. He was protective of his sister and yet allowed her to tag along with him when he would join up with his peers to play tag, climb trees and play riotous games of hide-and-seek. When Toni and Fred were children, and the growing Rossi family had moved to their new house on Victoria Road, the area consisted of largely undeveloped fields and forests. Aside from the usual childhood scrapes and bruises, safety from strangers was not an issue. Would that were the case today, Toni thought, being aware not only of "stranger danger" but monsters that lurked a lot closer to home.

Fred seemed to delight in his younger sister's intelligence and beauty, and as Toni matured into her teens and early adulthood, he was protective and keenly aware of her attractiveness to the opposite sex. He tried to steer her clear of what he knew to be the pitfalls of adolescent male interest, advising and protecting her as much as he could. However, when Toni fell into the clutches of James, as Fred always thought of what happened, all he could do was stand by and watch his sister sink into the slough of despondency and catch her before she fell too far. He knew about bad choices, did Fred, and he was certain that James was a narcissistic charlatan, and that Toni would be badly hurt. However, he could do little but watch as the nightmare that was Toni's marriage to James unfolded.

Confiding in Toni about his own marital problems was a relief that he tried not to take advantage of too often. He was determined not to burden her unnecessarily, especially after the dark days of her own marriage were finally over. However, Toni's absolute love and openness with Fred made him turn to her when he needed to. She made him "pinkie-swear" that when the need arose, he would let her know. Siblings forever...

Now, as Fred sat alone in his office, worrying about his marriage and the safety of his young children, he felt as though his only recourse was to talk to his sister and let her know how far things had unraveled in his household. He dialed Toni's number, hoping that she was available to talk with him. He combed his fingers through his hair while he waited to hear her voice.

Toni knew that Fred's marriage was not all that he had hoped it would be. He had met Laura when her parents were in the process of having a new home built on the outskirts of Arkell, east of Guelph. She was pretty, blonde and flirtatious with the newly minted owner of Rossi Construction, and Fred allowed himself to be beguiled, against his better judgment. She was warmly accepted into Fred's family, who let out a collective sigh of relief that their handsome, personable twenty-seven-year-old bachelor son had finally found someone with whom he could settle down. They seemed willing to ignore Laura's youth (she was twenty-one when she and Fred met) and her occasional petulance when things didn't go the way she wanted. And her not well-hidden predilection for drink.

Toni answered the phone after a few rings, her warm, husky

voice filling Fred's heart with relief. "Hi Freddo, I've been thinking about you and wondering how things are going. It's great to hear from you!"

Fred tried to keep the worry out of his voice when he told her how relieved he was to hear her voice. "I'm afraid things aren't going well at home, Toni, and I just needed to hear your voice." He tried not to sound as pathetic as he felt.

However, his sister knew him well and voiced her concern.

"Fred, talk to me... What's happening? You don't sound good." Fred, partly undone by her concern, found it hard to speak.

"Freddie, take your time, start at the beginning. I'm here and listening."

Toni's words had their usual effect on her brother. He always found her so darn easy to talk to, no matter what was happening. Even in their early teens, she was able to coax her brother into confiding in her and he was always afraid that he would wear out his welcome in that respect. However, she assured him repeatedly that he would always have her attention and love, no matter what.

As he began telling his sister about his concerns, he found himself relaxing into the warmth of her attention, knowing that she would treat him with respect and that no confession would find its way to anyone else's ears. Little wonder to her brother that she was always in demand as a therapist.

"I don't like bothering you, Toni, but I don't know where else to turn. I'm sure that it comes as no surprise that things aren't good with Laura and me. I've tried to keep her drinking problems out of sight as best I can. I must confess that I can still be beguiled by Laura's charm and her promise that 'it will never happen again, Freddie, honest!' A precursor of things to come occurred on our wedding night when, at the end of the evening, I went looking for my bride and found her pasted against my best friend, Charlie, slow-dancing to a hurtin' country-and-western oldie. Charlie, seeing me approach, had the grace to immediately relinquish Laura, who stumbled into my arms, slurring the words, 'Love ya, honey…' Charlie later told me that Laura had insisted on dancing with him and that it seemed easier to go along with her than to deny her request, drunk as she was. He apologized to me profusely. I had no problem accepting his apology, knowing that any blame was not his."

Fred told Toni that their relationship seemed to improve as the newly-weds settled into a routine of work, domestic routines and the news of their first pregnancy, unexpected but welcomed by all, especially the older Rossis, who had been eagerly anticipating the onset of grandparenthood.

"As you know, Toni, Laura's pregnancy was not an easy one, and she blamed me for the loss of her figure, varicose veins, nightly trips to the washroom and unpredictable moods. I often found solace on the couch in the den where I could be assured of a few hours of uninterrupted sleep. Laura's mother, June, seemed to be visiting her daughter more often, and when not in residence with me and Laura, would call Laura several times a day to make sure all was well. I would catch Laura in conversation with her mother first thing in the morning. "I'm fine, Mom. Yup, I'm just going downstairs now to get something out of the freezer. Okay… I'll call you when I get back upstairs."

"These conversations would go on throughout the day, mother and daughter seemingly caught in some sort of nexus from which neither could, nor wanted to escape. I had hoped that once the baby was born, June would back off a bit and tend to her own husband, George. George is, as you know, a large, taciturn fellow, who never has much to say to anyone and seems perfectly content to allow his wife to run their lives however she wants.

"Georgie, our baby, rapidly developed a case of seemingly unending colic. His screams reverberated throughout the house all night and into the morning, when he and his mother would fall into a stupor for a few hours. The screaming would then begin again.

"The only person that Georgie calmed down with was our mama, who would arrive as soon as she could most days to take over Georgie's care until I came home after work, exhausted but ready to assume the burden of my apoplectic son. I know that Mama would tell you about June's habit of a 'few glasses of wine to calm me down, don't you know' after lunch. And I also know how upset Mama would be, but she didn't know what to do or say about it. Laura also seemed to partake in this ritual more and more as the days went by. I had been aware that June drank, but I didn't realize that Laura was joining her mother in the afternoon ritual. When I attempted to talk about it with Laura, she raged at me for hours, blaming me for all of the ills of her life and then some. I was loath to bring the subject up again.

"Georgie finally tapered off in the colic department, and by the age of six months had become a large, bouncy baby, who gurgled and smiled at everyone within range. He loves his parents and his two doting grandmothers, who are thoroughly smitten with their personable grandson."

Shortly thereafter, Laura discovered she was pregnant again. And that's when the real trouble began, Fred confided in Toni.

Toni took a moment to digest what Fred had told her. She tried to keep her personal feelings at bay. It pained her to hear her brother in so much distress.

However, Toni was certain that no one knew the extent of the problems nor the toll they were taking on her brother.

Fred mistook his sister's silence and said, "I'm so sorry to burden you with this, Toni. I'm ashamed that things have deteriorated so badly. I have suggested repeatedly that it might help for us to talk to someone, but Laura always becomes angry when I mention therapy, so I've stopped. I'm at a loss."

"Freddo, you are never a burden to me, ever. If anything, I am feeling awful that I was unaware of how bad things are. You should not have to shoulder all of this alone. I should have been more sensitive to what was happening. I knew that Mama was upset about the drinking, but I was hoping, as was she, that it was temporary. It's clearly not. However, blaming myself is not helping you.

"Give me a bit of time and let me think about what can be done to help. As I'm sure you know, therapists should never attempt to ply their wares on their own families. We are too close to the problems and cannot see the forest for the trees, as they say. It is why people with concerns are always wise to seek help from a professional, one who is neutral and can look at problems without the emotional involvement that comes with being part of the family. I will get back to you as soon as I can, promise."

"Thanks so much, Toni. As usual, telling you about what's been happening has made me feel better already. I will sleep better tonight knowing that you are willing to help. Bottom of my heart, sis!"

Chapter 8

Bruce decided to retrieve his truck from Viv after she told him that he should come and get it. He sat in the truck for a moment, trying to decide the best way to approach Viv, to try and win her back once and for all. The distraction of Sheila was just that: a distraction. He certainly enjoyed their time together, but his real goal was to reunite with Viv by any means he could. He'd not been sleeping or eating much and he needed to get his life back on track. And, to make matters worse, his clients were becoming increasingly annoyed at his appointment cancellations.

Roxie had called him the day before. "Bruce, I need to know when you will reschedule your client appointments for this week. I've had five phone calls this morning, and I don't think I can keep making excuses for you any longer. Please give me some idea about when you will be in the office."

Bruce tried to keep his reply light and non-committal. "I'll let you know as soon as I can, Rox. I'm in the process of finalizing a few things here, but I promise that as soon as I can see my way clear, you'll be the first to know. Keep up the good work, cutie." Roxie started to sputter at the inappropriate nickname, but Bruce disconnected the call before she could berate him.

He couldn't help it, after all – he felt like his life was spinning out of control. The separation from Viv was driving him crazy, to say nothing of the conversation he'd had with Peter, his cousin's husband. It had happened after his cousin Cynthia's funeral.

Bruce had called Peter to find out how he was doing and to fill him in with what was happening between him (Bruce) and Viv. "I'm glad you called, Bruce. I am having a hard time adjusting to Cynthia's death, even though we all knew it was inevitable. Her life-long smoking habit made the end a foregone conclusion. Her mother died the same way. I had prayed that taking care of her mother in her last few months would have convinced her to quit that awful habit, but it didn't. Oh, she made some attempts over the years, but none of them worked. She tried nicotine patches, gum-chewing, meetings, even therapy. Nothing worked. She suffered every winter from bronchitis. When she was hospitalized a few months ago with pneumonia, the doctors discovered her lung cancer. No surprise there. Oddly enough, the only person who was surprised was Cynthia. She figured that her attempts at quitting had somehow benefitted her and had staved off the inevitable.

"I had a good friend who experienced the same type of disbelief. He had spent his life as a pilot for the RCAF. The stories he told of hard-drinking and smoking and so on were hilariously funny at the time. However, the behavior inevitably caught up with him. He survived a heart attack but died of esophageal cancer. I saw him a month or so before his death, his voice a hoarse whisper. He looked at me and said, a puzzled look on his face, 'I don't know what happened. I gave up smoking two years ago.' He had somehow blocked out the fact that more than fifty years of non-stop smoking and drinking might take their toll on his health."

Now Peter said, "I'll be here, Bruce. We need to talk."

When Bruce pulled up in front of Peter and Cynthia's home, he noticed how neglected the front gardens looked. His cousin had been an enthusiastic gardener – no matter what she planted, everything responded to her touch and care with voluptuous abandon. Peter must be having a hard time of it, Bruce thought. Sure enough, when Peter answered the door, he looked even more haggard than he had at the funeral a few weeks before. Bruce tried to hug him, but Peter stepped out of reach and walked into the living room. He sat down heavily in one of the upholstered chairs. Bruce noted the used coffee cups on the end tables, papers strewn on the sofa. He could see into the kitchen area, which looked even more chaotic than where they were sitting.

"So, Pete, how's it going?" Bruce tried for levity in his tone but was afraid he fell short because his own problems were front and center in his whirling mind.

Peter wiped his hand over his face and stared at Bruce for a moment.

"I won't beat around the bush, Bruce." His voice cracked a bit. "Cynthia and I had some very frank discussions toward the end. She told me things about her childhood that were, honestly, disturbing, to put it mildly. She said that she regretted not telling me earlier but that she wanted to set the record straight, once and for all. She also said that she regretted not contacting a lawyer about what she told me. She made me promise that I would tell you what we talked about."

Peter looked directly into Bruce's eyes while he spoke. Bruce, in an attempt to forestall what he was afraid was inevitable, tried to appear innocent of any knowledge about what Peter might say, and spluttered, "Whatever do you mean, Peter?"

"Don't play the buffoon, Bruce – no amount of denial or other bullshit will let you off the hook this time." Again, he stared at Bruce with a look of pure disgust. "Cynthia told me what really happened all those years ago."

Bruce had always maintained, to family and friends alike, that when his father had been killed in a car accident, their mother had moved the three of them, Bruce, Cynthia and herself, to Toronto and made the best life she could, renting out rooms in their home and holding down a full-time job. Cynthia had been living with them since her parents had been killed in a freak boating accident on Lake Simcoe. The children, Bruce and Cynthia, fended for themselves most of the time. Bruce had told everyone that he left home voluntarily when he was sixteen to stay with his maternal grandparents and work. He met and married his first wife when he was twenty-two.

The real story, one that Bruce had never acknowledged to anyone, including himself, was markedly different. It had become apparent to his mother, and to others in the family, that Bruce, from an early age, was exhibiting a distinctly sexual interest in his young cousin, to the point that if Bruce entered a room where Cynthia was, she would start screaming, stopping only when Bruce left the room. Her aunt was disturbed and puzzled by her niece's behavior and unaware of its cause until one day she saw Bruce chase Cynthia, grab her by the arm and try to shove his hand up her skirt. That's when his mother knew she had to act.

She decided to remove Cynthia out of harm's way, and Cynthia spent most of the next several years with her aunt's best friend, who lived some distance from Toronto. When Cynthia was in her early teens, the decision was made to remove Bruce from the home and bring Cynthia back to live with her aunt. The decision was made more urgent when Bruce's behavior became even more outrageous and Bruce was sent to live with his grandparents.

It wasn't enough of a separation, apparently. When Cynthia

was fifteen and Bruce nineteen, he sexually abused and raped his cousin. The family somehow managed to deal with the aftermath, and Cynthia married an older man and had a son when she was sixteen. The truth about Will's parentage was never hinted at in the family until Cynthia told Peter, shortly before her death. The family, including Bruce, had welcomed Will, as it would any other member of the family, and the truth of his conception was never mentioned.

Bruce played the role of "uncle" with as much aplomb as any borderline personality could, which is to say, sporadically, at best. Sufferers of this disorder are hard-pressed to attend to any other people except themselves. There isn't enough energy left over. His relationship with his cousin was strained, at best.

Viv, his wife, was aware that something negative had happened in earlier days. She had asked Bruce about it a few times. "You and Cynthia seem to avoid each other, Bruce. And when you are together, I've noticed that your conversations seem strained and awkward. It's been this way since I've known you, and I can't figure out what's wrong."

Bruce, as usual, avoided addressing the question, turning it into a joke. "It's nothing, Viv. Just a carry-over from when we were kids. My mom always favored Cynthia, and so I got in the habit of teasing my cousin about it. I guess she still doesn't think it's as funny as I do. When my mom turfed me out of the house and I had to bunk in with my grandparents, I was pretty pissed off at her and Cynthia. We kind of avoided each other for a long time. But things are good, sweetheart, and it's nothing to be concerned about now. C'mere, and I'll show you how good they are." The last bit was said with an exaggerated leer.

Bruce now looked at his brother-in-law in stunned silence. His mind was racing with denials, his usual method of not taking responsibility for anything he was reluctant to admit. It was always someone else's doing, responsibility, etcetera. But Bruce had come to the last of the innocence cards, it appeared. He honestly had no idea that Will was his son. Or, more accurately, his mind had skittered away all those years, not acknowledging the obvious, that Will's birth had occurred less than a year after Bruce's "troubles" at home. It appeared that now, the jig was up.

Peter didn't say anything for a few moments. Then he said, "Are you going to tell Viv the truth now, or shall I?"

Bruce physically recoiled, blurting out, "No, no... I'll tell her."

He had absolutely no intention of doing anything of the sort. Bad enough that Viv had caught him red-handed, as it were, on several occasions, with his large hand on someone's leg or brushing his arm against someone's breast "by mistake". He'd always been able to laugh it off, allaying her fears, he thought, about his real intentions. And why couldn't he have whomever he wanted, really? He'd got away with all kinds of surreptitious behaviors his whole life. He certainly didn't intend to behave differently now. Besides, he couldn't help being tempted by those girls who deliberately provoked him with their short skirts, cleavages just waiting to be caressed.

Viv had always known that Bruce had a hard time keeping his hands to himself. She had caught him "red-handed" on a few occasions. One night, they were playing Scrabble with a good friend, Nancy. Nancy was sitting across the table from Viv, and Bruce was at the head of the table. Viv suddenly realized that Bruce was leaning over toward Nancy. Viv immediately knew what Bruce was doing. She said, "Bruce, take your hand off Nancy's leg, please."

Nothing was said. Bruce sat up, his hands on the table.

Nancy looked gratefully at Viv. The next time Viv and Nancy were together, Nancy told Viv the rest of the story. Bruce had insisted on driving Nancy home that evening and tried to French-kiss Nancy as she left the car. Nancy said, "Stop it, Bruce. I am not interested in you in the slightest, and Viv is a good friend. You should be ashamed of yourself." She said that Bruce didn't look ashamed at all and drove off in a huff.

She said now, "I don't think I did anything to encourage him, Viv. I'm so sorry that this happened." Viv gave her friend a hug and said not to worry, that she would talk to Bruce.

"He has always been like this, unfortunately. I've tried to talk to him about it, telling him that gone are the days when men could get away with this sort of sexual harassment – the touching, petting, hugs that lasted too long, pats on the bum, etcetera. Women are beginning to understand that these types of incidents are no longer seen as "men will be men." We are drawing the line at personal assault, no matter what the "intentions" are, and that if he insisted on continuing this type of behavior, he would run up against the law and worse. Unfortunately, he's not getting it. I am so sorry that you were subjected to this awful behavior."

After Viv and Bruce separated, she was actually approached by several other women who had similar stories to tell about their experiences with Bruce. Their stories only served to reinforce her decision to leave her husband, as quickly as possible. If she could.

Now Bruce got up abruptly from his seat in Peter's living room and moved hastily toward the front door. Peter called out to him as Bruce turned the door knob. "Make sure you tell Viv what we talked about, Bruce, because if you don't, I swear I will."

Chapter 9

Bruce remembered how he had longed for his mom to spend more time with him when he was a young child. His only playmate was his younger cousin, Cynthia. She was okay, but she was just a girl and made it obvious that she didn't want to have anything to do with him most of the time. He really liked chasing her around the house when his mom wasn't home, pretending to try and pull his cousin's panties off, hearing her screams. If his mom happened to be home, she would run toward the pair, yelling at Bruce to "leave Cynthia alone, or you'll get a lickin'!" The "lickin" never happened, but at least he had his mom's attention for a while.

And negative attention was almost as satisfying as the positive kind, at least in Bruce's mind.

Bruce's mom was at her wit's end when Bruce's behavior was out of control. She was also too busy trying to hold things together and hadn't time to develop close friendships with other women. She had no one with whom she could confide when things were bad. And she didn't know anyone who was a single mom with two young kids, one of whom seemed determined to drive her around the bend.

Her only recourse was her parents, but she hated to bother them. Her dad was strictly old-school when it came to discipline, and Gloria knew instinctively that "beating the crap" out of Bruce wouldn't lead to better behavior. She had watched her brothers suffer under that approach and knew the consequences in later life: bad marriages, drinking binges and various other mental health problems. Still, she had never encountered anyone like her son and his behavior.

Her own mother, appalled by Bruce's shenanigans, seemed to blame her daughter for the behavior. "If you were just stricter with him, dear, I'm sure he would straighten out," she remonstrated after one of Bruce's episodes. "I know that your dad would just get out the switch and teach your brothers a thing or two. And if that didn't work, being sent to their room without supper did the trick."

Gloria begged to differ with her parents' approach. "The last time I sent him to his room, Mother, he smashed both the inside window and the storm window in his bedroom. Then he used a piece of the broken glass to cut his arm open. I don't think your approach would work with Bruce. Not only did I have to pay a doctor to stitch up his arm but I had to have both windows replaced."

And, she didn't add, that episode did nothing to improve Bruce's behavior.

She went on, "When one of Bruce's older male cousins was working around our house, mowing grass, for example, Bruce would sneak up behind him and scare the living daylights out of him. I sure didn't like that, either, and neither did the cousin. Eventually, the cousins stopped helping me, undoubtedly because of Bruce's pestering. I also had the feeling that their not helping me any more was exactly what Bruce wanted. Fine with me, he seemed to think. Now I can have my mom all to myself."

A day of reckoning came when Bruce, age fifteen, saw his mom relaxing on the living room couch, reading a magazine. Bruce, without thinking of what the consequences might be, ran silently toward his mom and pushed her back onto the couch's pillows while trying to kiss her and feel her breasts. What followed was not what Bruce had hoped. His mom shrieked and shoved Bruce off her and onto the floor and ran for the telephone. She called her parents and explained what had just happened.

Her dad, a very tall, dour, Presbyterian sort of person, arrived shortly, picked his grandson up by the scruff of his neck and took him out to the car. No words were exchanged. Bruce was given a pillow and a blanket and was allowed to sleep on the stair landing, given three meals a day and many chores to do around his grandparents' house.

When he was nineteen, Bruce snuck back into his mother's house and sexually assaulted and raped his cousin.

At that point, the entire family closed their doors and hearts against him. He found a hostel to sleep at and a job in the plumbing department at City Hall.

Bruce learned quickly to charm and dissemble in order to get what he wanted, turning negative assessments about his misdeeds into jokes. He worked his way up into the social services department by means of his gift of the gab, filling in the holes of his resume with vague half-truths. He managed to sweet-talk his way into the dwellings and arms of many of his clients, eventually securing the heart of a young, ambitious blonde named Shelley. Shelley worked two jobs so that Bruce could attend university and graduate school. Bruce returned his wife's hard work by having a year-long affair with her sister.

As he was finishing up his graduate degree in social work, Viv came into his life, and Bruce concocted an alternate story about his past.

Chapter 10

After spending the morning with regular clients, Toni left her office on Woolwich and drove down Gordon Street. She passed the old limestone-and-brick homes that lined the street, many set off by decades-old maple trees, now flaunting autumn's brilliant scarlets and golds. The smell of the leaves as they lay on the sidewalks always reminded her of school starting, new beginnings, hope and the limitless choices of youth. Funny how the more paths you choose in life, the fewer choices you actually have as you get older, she thought.

Speaking of choice, she turned her thoughts to the clients she'd be seeing that afternoon at the University of Guelph's Sexual Education Centre. She was a volunteer counselor at the center one afternoon a week. Ever since she'd had an abortion a few years ago, she was committed to helping other women with similar dilemmas.

As she pulled into the parking lot behind the University Center, she noticed the regular group of anti-abortion protestors standing across the street, shouting at people who were going into the building. Several held posters of gruesomely mangled fetuses. These photos were purportedly true renderings of hospital abortion procedures. If they hadn't been so horrifying to look at, Toni would have laughed at them. Nothing could be further from the truth in terms of the reality of an abortion. However, most people had no knowledge of the procedure, and many believed what was portrayed in the posters.

Toni suddenly spotted a familiar profile among the protestors. No, she thought, it can't be. She swerved to avoid a student on a bicycle. I'm seeing things. 'Time for a reality check, Antonia.' She parked her car and looked at the group of protestors again, but the person she'd seen had disappeared. She locked her car and headed toward the Sex Ed Centre through the back of the building.

When the elevator doors opened onto the third floor, she turned left toward an unmarked door at the end of the hallway. Even though a security guard patrolled the lobby, occasionally a protestor would get by him and find his or her way to the third floor. Calls to the campus police were not an uncommon occurrence. Too many abortion clinics and providers were targets of some of the more crazed protestors of the political and "moral" right.

"Hi, Donna," Toni greeted the receptionist as she headed toward the counseling room. Donna returned her greeting, handed her several phone messages, then turned back to her computer. Suddenly, the door to the clinic burst open, and a student volunteer counselor rushed in, visibly upset.

"Amber, what's wrong?" Toni turned and moved quickly toward her.

"Toni," she gasped, hair messed, cheeks flushed, crying. "I've just been hassled by one of the protestors. He grabbed my arm and tried to stop me from coming into the building. I kicked him in the shin with my boot, and he let go of my arm but not before he screamed obscenities at me. He had these wild-looking eyes. As if he were stoned... or crazy."

Toni led her over to the windows that overlooked the front of the building. "Do you see him down there?" Amber peered out at the group still milling about on the sidewalk. She shook her head, no.

"Could you describe him to the police?"

"No problem – he wasn't the typical protestor. He was tall, thin, with a long dark ponytail. Aside from his weird eyes, rather aristocratic-looking, actually. He didn't seem to belong to the usual crowd out there."

"Donna," Toni said to the receptionist who had overheard their conversation, "please phone security and have them send someone up right away. Let's get some water, Amber, and sit in my office while we wait." She was now convinced that the person she'd glimpsed outside and the man who had tried to assault Amber were the same person. James. What in the world was happening to him? She'd have to talk to him this evening at dinner.

The rest of the afternoon kept Toni busy, dealing with Amber, security, and several clients. She didn't have time to worry about James, for which she was grateful. She stopped at the variety store on Yorkshire to get cat food and wondered if Bruce had made it home to his lonely feline. I'll have to meet with him as soon as possible, she thought. Both James and Bruce seemed to be disintegrating before her eyes. And now Fred's marriage. Thank God for Hank.

As she drove toward her house, she saw a woman step out of a sleek black car in front of their house on Glasgow Street. Toni didn't recognize her. She slowed her car down and watched as the woman stepped onto the front porch and rang the doorbell. She was stunning. Tall, slender, with olive skin, long black hair in a single braid down her back. She was wearing what looked like a very expensive aubergine-colored pant suit. Casual, but very classy. Suddenly, the front door opened, and Hank reached out to this woman and pulled her into an embrace.

They entered the house together and the door closed behind them.

Toni was so shocked that she nearly side-swiped a car parked illegally on the street. She managed to pull into her driveway and sat in the car, engine off, her mind spinning. Who the hell was that, she wondered? She entered the house by the side door and as she did, she could hear the faint sounds of laughter coming from upstairs and one of Hank's favorite jazz CDs. Now even more puzzled and beginning to feel upset, she saw the message light on the phone, blinking. She listened to the message.

"Hi, my sweet," Hank's deep rumble sounded. "Just want to give you an update on the alarm guy. He checked everything out and couldn't find any problems. Said the guy must be some kind of pro to be able to by-pass this system. Anyway, on to plan B, the panic alarm. I'm busy tonight, but I'll see you tomorrow. *Ciao, bella.*"

You certainly are busy, thought Toni. Dismay flooded through her, threatening to overwhelm all her great, positive emotions about him. Wait a minute, Antonia, her rational side chided. What can you expect? You're the one who called a halt to any further emotional involvement, my dear. The guy's not a saint. How long do you expect him to cool his heels (and everything else)? No one mentioned the "M" word, here. Monogamy was never discussed. After all, he's just a man.

"Shut up!" Toni shook her head violently, trying to dislodge her alter ego from her mind. "This is all your fault, James, you creep. Will I ever be able to trust men again?" There has to be some explanation for what I saw, she thought. She heard the front door of the old house close again, and she positioned herself behind the curtain in the living room's bay window that overlooked Glasgow Street.

Hank opened the passenger door for the woman, walked around the car, got into the driver's seat, started the car and drove off. *He must be pretty good friends with her, whoever she is,* Toni thought. *He's driving her car. He's also wearing some pretty cool clothes himself. Wonder where they're going? Okay, Toni, stop speculating and get yourself going.*

She spent some time selecting her clothes for her dinner with James. When they'd spoken by phone earlier, he'd apologized for his surprise visit and said that he wanted to make up for his unwarranted behavior. She wanted to look good without giving her ex-husband any wrong ideas. She selected a dark-green cashmere sweater set and matching trousers, discreet gold earrings and watch.

Nothing ostentatious, just her usual understated elegance. She twisted her long dark hair up into a knot on her head, small tendrils of curls escaping as usual. She fed Humphrey, set the alarm and headed for dinner on Yarmouth Street.

She loved this restaurant, The Other Brother's, and the building it was in.

As a university student, she had come here to dine only on special occasions – her finances were most often limited to an occasional pub meal – but would walk past the lovely old yellow-brick building, admiring its historic architecture. The restaurant, then called La Cucina, was where she had meals with her parents on special occasions. Later on, she and James treated themselves during the early days of their brief marriage. Not all of her memories were happy ones. She recalled their last evening there.

"What now, James? How long do you have before you have to leave the university?" She had fiddled with the stem of her wine glass, curious about his response, not wanting to believe that this crisis was happening, longing to yell and scream at him;

too much in control to do so.

His answer was perfectly Jamesian: arrogant, slightly abusive, dismissive and superior. "The small minds of the faculty disciplinary committee have decreed that I am to be relieved of my duties immediately. My salary, naturally, will continue until the end of term. I shall have to see what other universities will benefit from a resident Restoration specialist." His voice, articulate and cold, matched his bony nose, unsmiling eyes and thin lips. And to think she once loved him.

"And you, my dear? Will you be the dutiful wife and follow your temporarily disgraced husband to wherever?"

"James. We've discussed this many times. You know I'm not going to leave my work here, or my family." Toni had begun her therapy practice the year before and was committed to both her private clients and to her volunteer work at the university clinic. Even more importantly, she had realized for a long time that their marriage was a colossal mistake that no amount of dutiful behavior would make right. Her pregnancy, the discovery of irreversible abnormalities, James' unforgiving rage at her suggestion of terminating the pregnancy, all contributed to her loss of positive feelings for him.

She might have decided differently had the final blow not befallen their marriage. James was accused by three students of sexual improprieties. He denied the allegations, not with bitterness, but with his typical air of Machiavellian superiority. Couldn't understand what all the fuss was about. After all, he was James Barrington the Third. His very air of entitlement only served to undermine any hope of leniency on the part of the university's disciplinary body.

"Well, my dear, your loss, of course. The other drones at the university will view your defection with self-satisfied smugness.

May you be happy with them." He had raised his glass in a mock toast.

She remembered the rest of the evening, the subsequent weeks, as a blur of minimal explanations to family and friends (no surprise or dismay there) and legal obligations. Work became a welcome panacea. She felt little but relief at his departure and a sense of unending exhaustion. She knew it was her mind's way of dealing with grief, but it surprised her, nonetheless. When she was able to rouse herself to action, she had found herself standing on the steps of 224 Glasgow Street North, an "apartment for rent" ad in hand. Her life there had been peaceful in comparison and Hank's friendship and their growing attraction to each other wonderful bonuses.

Now she parked her car and walked back toward the old sewing factory building that housed the restaurant. As she ascended the few steps to the door, she straightened her small shoulders and forced a smile, determined to push negative thoughts away. "Go get 'em!" whispered her inner voice.

"Good evening, Dr. Rossi," Mario, the maître'd said as she handed him her suede coat. "You are looking *molta bella* tonight."

Toni blushed at the compliment, charmed as always by his Sicilian accent, so similar to her parents. "*Grazie*, Mario. I'm meeting someone – he has a long dark ponytail. Has he arrived yet?"

"*Si, Signora*. Follow me." As they made their way through the crowded restaurant, she noticed a very familiar profile in the back corner of the main room. So this is where they came. Hank and his date. 'Stop it,' Toni.

She saw James rising from his seat as she and Mario approached. Mario pulled out her chair for her, but Toni stopped him. She wasn't going to spend the next two hours or so looking at Hank and his gorgeous friend. She stood beside James and asked if he would mind sitting in her seat. He looked at her quizzically then moved toward the other side of the table. As he did so, she noticed him limping.

"What happened to your leg?" she asked.

"Nothing," he replied. "A small altercation with a coffee table." Changing the subject, he said, "You look lovely as always, my dear. I've taken the liberty of ordering your favorite wine." He still remembers my favorite wine? thought Toni, with dismay.

The waiter hovered, sleeve draped with a linen napkin, to pour a red Barolo. James, correct to a fault, held the wine glass up to view it, lowered the glass under his nose to smell it, then sipped a small amount. Only when he was satisfied did he turn to the patient waiter and say, dismissively, "fine."

Toni remembered the early days when she had found James' public behavior sophisticated. Now she saw it for what it was: condescending and elitist. Try to control yourself, she thought. He asked you here for a reason, and you can use this time to your advantage if you can keep your level of irritability low to nonexistent.

"So, James, how have you been these last few years? How's Northern Alberta?" She noticed again that his skin had a grayish pallor and that several serious-looking pimples had sprouted on his face.

He told her amusing anecdotes about the northern town, its inhabitants and university faculty. According to James, most of the latter were either intellectually defective, boring, or both.

They made small talk through the hors d'oeuvres and the main course. He seemed to have some problem eating and swallowing. The bites he took were tiny, his rate of eating very slow. By the time Toni had finished her entrée, he had barely made a dent in his. When she questioned his appetite, he said he wasn't hungry, his throat was sore, and again changed the subject.

As they drank their espresso, Toni asked him if he was seeing anyone special. She was genuinely curious; she had loved him for a while.

He looked at her sadly and said that there had been someone, for a time, but that it hadn't been the right relationship for him, and that it was over. He leaned forward, took Toni's hand in his and said, "No one has ever been able to erase you from my heart, dear Antonia." He met her eyes unflinchingly.

Oh, dear, she thought. Wait, she cautioned herself. Be nice, be sympathetic, but don't give an inch. He did look so wistful, so charming and almost boyish at that moment. "I'm sorry, James." She really was – sorry that she'd asked about romance. She'd know better next time. Next time? There wouldn't be one, of course.

They retrieved their coats and bid goodnight to Mario. Toni quickly looked to where Hank and his friend had been sitting, but the table was occupied by another couple.

Toni offered to give James a ride to wherever he was staying, and he directed her to the hotel on Gordon Street, just east of the university. As they passed the university's darkened buildings, Toni asked him if by some chance he'd been on campus that day. He bristled at her question, replying that he wouldn't be caught dead on that two-bit campus again. She found his refusal to admit to his behavior unnerving. She didn't pursue her questioning.

She pulled into the parking lot in front of the hotel and stopped the car, waiting for James to say goodnight. "Lovely to see you, my dear. I'll be in touch soon." He leaned toward her and kissed her cheek.

She pulled out of the parking lot before she realized that James had left his coat on the front seat. She drove back to the parking lot of the hotel, intending to leave the coat for him at the front desk. As she got out of her car, she saw James limp toward a waiting taxi. He got in and the taxi drove off.

Chapter 11

James settled into the seat of the taxi, thinking about his dinner with Toni. His shin was throbbing, and he rubbed the injured area with his hand. Christ, that hurt, he thought, remembering the look of anger on the face of the student he'd tried to prevent from entering the building that afternoon.

She'd tried to engage him. "Those photos are ridiculous, you know. Why are you trying to scare people with them?" She told him that the photo he was waving was wrong and that abortions were nothing like what the poster portrayed. He was so angry that he grabbed her by the arm.

He had no idea what his next step might be, but before he had a chance to react, the student kicked him with the pointed toe of her boot, wiping all thought of retort from his mind. Before he could react, she'd wrenched her arm away from him and ran for the building's entrance. Before she disappeared, she yelled back at him, "I'm going to call the police!" He knew better than to follow and melted into the crowd of protesters around him. The last thing he needed was to be targeted by the campus police.

Now he watched out the taxi window as the Arboretum passed by in the night. He passed his hand over his face, trying not to rupture the pustules that kept forming each day. He knew he looked awful, but the way he looked was the least of his concerns. He paid the taxi driver and hobbled up the short walkway to his house. Once inside, he sank into one of the living room chairs. His dinner with Toni had been successful, he thought. She seemed less mistrustful and a bit more conciliatory than before. He would have to work on whatever charm he could muster when he was in her presence. His goal was to win her trust back and to convince her that spending time with him was a good thing. He knew that it might take him a while to do this, and time was becoming an increasingly precious commodity for him.

He gazed at the photo of Tim that he kept on the small table beside him. "God, I miss you," James thought. "We were so good together. We just didn't have enough time."

Tim had been one of his graduate students at the University of Guelph.

He'd had the good fortune of owning a small house on St. George's Hill, courtesy of his parents, who decided that buying instead of renting a house for their son made financial sense. Whenever they could, James and he retreated to Tim's home to "work on Tim's Ph.D. thesis". That's the excuse he'd used with his wife, Toni.

When Tim became ill with the disgusting disease that threatened to do away with much of the male population of homosexuals in the late twentieth century, James vowed to stay with Tim until the end.

They had time to talk about that end. Before it occurred for Tim, their discussions became more detailed. James had initially encouraged Tim to take advantage of the new anti-viral drugs and treatments available. However, Tim had other ideas in mind.

Over a period of time, he convinced James that the only way forward for the two lovers was to suffer through to the end of their current lives in order to be reunited in the hereafter.

"Don't you see, James?" Tim said, pleading with his lover, who was newly diagnosed with the same virus. "What happens to us in the here and now is painful but brief. What counts is our reunion in the great beyond, where we can be reunited forever without judgment from those who refuse to understand our type of love.

"We can finally be free to be together, without shame, into eternity."

James, distraught beyond reason at the thought of losing his love, reluctantly agreed. After his initial shock at the idea of an early, agonizing death, he came to share Tim's idea of a second life together in the never-ending future. He was now impatient for his end here on earth and longing for the reunion with his great love.

James had one last task to accomplish before that glorious meeting could happen.

When the end came for Tim, slowly and agonizingly, James' position at the university also ended, and he left for a much less prestigious position at a much inferior school. At least that was how he thought of Athabasca. However, knowing what lay ahead for him, whatever humiliation he had to suffer in the present was worth his knowledge of what the future held for him and Tim.

Fortunately for Toni, her physical relationship with James had ended before his involvement with Tim, so she avoided contracting the same disease. However, not in time to discover that she was at the very beginning of the pregnancy that became a burden and ended in termination. The discovery of her husband's infidelity and his subsequent removal from the University of Guelph faculty, along with the sexual harassment allegations against James, were the end of an increasingly painful marriage.

Much to James' surprise, Tim left his small house in Guelph to James. It was a bittersweet gift that James treasured. The memories of his dead lover comforted James and made him more determined than ever to bring his ex-wife as much pain as possible. The methods of accomplishing these things kept James occupied in his small house.

Chapter 12

Toni drove to her Saturday morning appointments. Few therapists in the city worked on weekends, but she and Bruce had decided that they would rather work Saturday mornings than work evenings during the week. Toni held her group for abused women on Saturday mornings in addition to a few regular clients.

As she pulled into the parking lot beside the old building which housed their clinic's offices, she noticed that Bruce's car was already in its usual spot. Good, she thought, maybe I'll have a chance to talk with him for a few minutes.

Something was obviously bothering him, and she needed to find out if she could help.

Given the speed with which Bruce met her at the front desk, he must have been looking out the office window, waiting for her arrival.

"You interfering bitch!" he began. His face was red and his fists were clenched by his sides. Conscious of the curious eyes of their waiting clients, Toni put a hand on Bruce's shoulder to lead him into her office. He swept her hand away.

"How dare you!" he continued. "How dare you and Viv enter my home without my permission!"

Toni flushed to her hairline. "Bruce – not here," she muttered. "Let's find somewhere private to talk, please?"

Bruce looked around the foyer. "These aren't my clients. They were" – he paused triumphantly – "yours." He addressed the three embarrassed women, members of Toni's Saturday morning group. "You see what kind of a person she really is? Take a good look..." He turned and pointed a shaking finger at Toni.

"Bruce, please..."

"I can't have a private life, is that it? You and Viv will be really lucky if I don't press charges against you."

Toni sat down beside one of her clients and folded her hands in her lap. She turned her face toward Bruce, tilting her head to give him her full attention in hopes that this would calm him down.

"Well, don't you have anything to say for yourself, Toni? I thought you were not only my partner but my friend, too."

Toni waited.

"Don't try your therapist crap on me!" He was sputtering with anger. "You have nothing to say, do you...? You've lost it, that's what's happened. Some professional." He was now pacing back and forth, glaring at her.

"Bruce, not here." Toni tried not to plead.

Bruce stopped in front of Toni and grabbed a handful of her hair, pulling her head back, pushing his sweating face close to hers. "Say it! You broke into my apartment because Viv's jealous and she talked you into going with her."

"Dr. Bruce..." The stunned face of a bald-headed man appeared at the door. "I..." he began to stutter.

Bruce dropped Toni's hair and stepped away from her. "Stay out of my personal life, Toni, or you will regret it." He brushed past his startled client.

"Mr. Holton, I can be with you in just a minute. I'll buzz Roxie." He ran up the stairs, two at a time, to his office.

Mr. Holton ran for the front door.

Toni stood and addressed her stunned clients. "I'm sorry that you saw this," she began, attempting to calm herself while diffusing the situation for her clients. "The doctor is having some personal problems." Giving out more details would not be appropriate at this time. Bruce's performance was bad enough, she thought.

Toni's three clients avoided looking at her, gathered their sweaters and purses and stepped quickly out the front door.

At that moment, two police officers arrived. "Our panic line went off at the station – is everything okay here?"

The other officer asked, "What's the problem?"

Toni exhaled. "I think we're okay, officer." Her clients disappeared around the building and into the parking lot as she spoke.

"No, we're not. I pushed the alarm," Roxie interrupted. "You need to talk to Dr. Patterson, upstairs…"

"Roxie," Toni began.

"He assaulted Dr. Rossi here," Roxie said. "I saw the whole thing. I'll give you a statement, but you'd better hurry upstairs before he escapes…"

The officers, hands on their holstered guns, went swiftly up the steps. The first officer at the top of the stairs shouted back, "He's gone!" As they descended the stairs where Toni and Roxie waited, the officer said, "He must've seen the cruiser and gone down the fire escape. The window behind his desk is wide open."

Toni and Roxie closed the office early after giving their statements to the police. There were to be no charges, Toni insisted, but the police, equally firmly, asked for contact information for the clients who had witnessed Bruce's assault. They said they would report back to Toni later that week.

Toni worried about what was happening to Bruce. She had seen some odd behavior over the years, but Bruce had always managed to cover up any slips with either a joke, an affronted denial, or a change of subject. Until now, his behaviors had not interfered with his work or with hers. She definitely had to figure out what was causing these enormous changes before Bruce did any further damage to himself or to their business.

For years, Toni and Viv had held to a Saturday lunch routine, and today was no exception. In fact, Toni knew that she had to discuss that morning's events with Viv. She stopped at Angelino's and picked out their favorites for lunch before heading to Viv's house on Metcalf.

Viv took the bag of food from Toni, peering inside the bag as she did so. "We can eat outside, Toni. It's a beautiful day and it may be one of the last of this year." She laid out the prosciutto, sliced provolone and asiago, olives and wholegrain bread. Toni had also bought two small, decadent desserts.

Viv noticed that something was troubling Toni. Her friend's hands were shaking as she took a sip of Pellegrino. Viv urged Toni to tell her what was bothering her. Toni gave her an abbreviated version of what had occurred that morning at the clinic.

Viv was appalled when Toni told her what happened. In fact, she said she had spoken to Bruce by phone just before the episode that morning. "He didn't sound angry," she said. In fact, he seemed pleased that she'd been so worried about him that she'd gone to his apartment.

She saw that Toni's hand holding her sandwich was trembling.

Toni reluctantly asked if Bruce had ever been violent with her. She hated having to ask that question, but Bruce's behavior that morning left her with no choice. She thought that she knew him. Clearly she didn't.

Viv answered the question by saying that Bruce had never been violent toward her, but that he had broken some things in their home when he was upset about something. She admitted that he'd thrown chairs at the ceiling occasionally and broken the back door as he slammed his way out of the house after an argument.

"But he's never hit me, Toni..." Viv sounded apologetic when she pointed out this questionable saving grace.

Toni knew that there was a very fine line between violence toward objects and violence toward people. She kept that thought to herself.

Viv saw how exhausted her friend was and had her lie down on the couch in front of the television. She covered her with a soft paisley blanket, and Toni dozed off while a *salade Nicoise* was being assembled on the Cooking Channel.

Chapter 13

When Toni woke up, she only had time to drive back to her house for Giuliana's present, splash on a little perfume and gel down some persistent curls around her face. No time to ruminate about that morning's events at the clinic or about the fact that Hank's car was not in the driveway. 'Gone again,' she thought, and with effort managed to clear her head of unpleasant thoughts, at least for the time being.

She drove to her parents' home on Grange Street. They had bought the small Ontario brick cottage when all their children had "flown from the nest", they said. Toni's childhood home, out on Victoria Road, was too large and too empty. The change seemed to agree with them. Their "new" house sat on the east side of St. George's Hill and their large lot was covered with every imaginable bit of horticulture, carefully tended and weed-free. Not even the most tenacious weeds would think of taking root on the Rossis' property.

As Toni parked behind several other cars in the wide driveway, she thought that her dad had missed his real calling in life. She'd never seen him as content as he was while puttering in his large vegetable gardens. Probably not having to fret over employees, plans, schedules and income helped, too. There was always something to do here, even in late fall – perennials to divide and give to family and friends, new stock to be protected from the Canadian winter, root vegetables to be harvested, pickled, canned and stored. And, just after Christmas, the new garden catalogues would arrive. Her parents would spend weeks poring over the booklets, making plans, lists and dreaming of the new season to come.

Toni was the last to arrive. Giuliana ran to the door and wrapped her arms around her aunt's legs. "I've been waiting!" she sang out, twirling in her imported party dress, face flushed, eyes shining. "Look, *Zia*, new shoes! From *Nonno*!"

Toni's father looked sheepish with pleasure.

Kisses and hugs were delivered to Toni's two sisters, brothers-in-law, brother Fred and her parents. Toni carried the little girl with her to the kitchen for a glass of wine.

"I'm tree, *Zia*, tree now!"

"*Tre, bambina*," Toni's mother corrected.

"Three," stressed Simonetta, Giuliana's mother. "Three."

They ate the sumptuous meal that Toni's mom had spent days planning and cooking, they gossiped, admired Giuliana and all her new outfits, played with her latest, most glamorous Barbie doll, and helped put the decals on the new bicycle exactly where she wanted them. When the doorbell rang, Toni was the one who opened the door.

Her hand flew to her cheek in shock. James stood on the front porch, a fancy bag tied with a large pink ribbon in his hand. Toni could feel the stunned silence of her family behind her.

"Hello, Antonia," James said, bending to kiss both her cheeks. "It's *Zia* Toni's new boyfriend," said Giuliana, running to the door.

"No, Giuli, no. Just an old friend." But the little girl wasn't listening.

"It's my birthday party – come in, come in," she said as she grabbed James by the hand.

James looked at Toni. She was having difficulty with this

sudden intrusion into her family life. How had this happened? She wondered. James addressed several family members, seeming to be nonplussed by the subdued greetings from the group.

"I don't mean to interrupt a pretty girl's birthday party," said James. "Here is your present, Giuliana. After I saw you at Tim Horton's this morning, I just had to bring this." He handed the bag to the excited little girl.

Simonetta, Giuliana's mother, intercepted the gift bag and tried to hand it back to James. "No, sorry, she can't take gifts from strangers."

"But Mama, he's not a stranger," said Giuliana. "*Nonna* knew him today. So did *Nonno*. They talked to him. They drank coffee together."

"I know all these people," James said. "I was married to your *Zia* Toni. Just ask her."

Toni nodded. Giuli took a heavy leather-bound book out of the gift bag and began to turn the lavishly illustrated pages. "There're lots of words." Disappointment in her voice.

"It's *Grimm's Fairy Tales.* You'll read them to her, won't you, Toni?" asked James, a hint of glee in his voice.

"Thank you, *Zio* James," Giuli said, hugging him around his legs.

He bent and kissed her head. "Thanks, Toni, too," he said. "I'll go now." He looked at Toni, and to her amazement, he was misty-eyed.

Toni leaned forward and quickly kissed him goodbye on the cheek. "Goodbye, James." She firmly shut the door after him. Her family stared at her for a long moment,

"No, Toni, don't even start – not for a minute…" This from Simonetta. "Cake time," said *Nonna*, firmly.

Chapter 14

Hank rolled his small suitcase along the line at the airport terminal, thinking about Toni and her current problems. He was reluctant to leave Guelph knowing that she was having troubles with both her partner and her ex-husband. However, at this point there was little he could do except offer support and phone her regularly.

She seemed to be handling things on her own, but he also knew it never hurt to listen and offer help if it was needed. And he had a feeling it would be needed at some point soon.

She had offered a bit of information about her current problems but seemed to prefer not to discuss them at length. He didn't like to pry, nor did he want those problems to be the focus of conversation when they were together. He decided that his best approach at the moment was to make sure she knew he was available and would help whenever he could. If he wasn't off on a book-signing trip, that is.

That left phone calls and assurances. He would see what he could find out about her ex-husband in Athabasca.

He settled himself into his seat on the plane, reading the itinerary that Stella, his agent, had sent. The week contained a lot of book signings at bookstores plus a spot on a morning TV show for young children. He always looked forward to meeting his fans when he could. There was no pretense among them, and their enthusiasm for his stories kept him writing more. He loved his interactions with his fans, whose average age was about seven.

One of his dreams was to have more children of his own. His teenage daughter was a blessing, but she was as busy as he, what with school and the distance from Guelph. He treasured their times together.

When he and his ex-wife, Aviva, were married, they vowed to have children.

Rachel's arrival was a joyous occasion in both their lives. However, as time passed, it became obvious to both parents that they had neither the time nor the inclination for more children. Aviva had finished her post-doc at the University of Guelph and was much in demand throughout the world of agronomy for advice and more, especially in the Middle East, Israel in particular, her place of birth. As her schedule became busier, Hank was forced to assume more parenting duties than before, and he found it difficult to attend to his job as reporter for the local newspaper, *The Guelph Mercury*.

When his first children's book was published and won a prestigious book award, he resigned his job and devoted himself to parenting and writing. Rachel loved having her Dad to herself, and Hank, when not changing diapers and running after his toddler, managed to carve out time each day to write. Looking back, it seemed to him a miracle that those years were as productive as they were. He would love to repeat the entire experience.

His and Aviva's marriage, however, wasn't as fortunate. It became obvious to them that both the distance and the separations were not beneficial to their relationship, and after a few years, they decided to divorce. There were few recriminations; the times apart and the distances showed the couple that it had become a marriage in name only. The impact on Rachel was minimal; she was accustomed to her mom's infrequent appearances. Divorce wasn't the traumatic event that it could be to children who lived full-time with both parents. Hank and Aviva remained in close contact with respect to Rachel and her development, and when Aviva was offered a full-time position in Toronto, their daughter traveled back and forth regularly until she began university in Toronto. Hank treasured his infrequent times with his daughter and was still a presence in his ex-wife's life occasionally, for dinners in Guelph or Toronto.

He had met someone after his divorce that he had hoped would be with him for the long haul. However, she had eventually made the decision to resume her relationship with her ex-partner and Hank had reluctantly said goodbye as graciously as possible. The antidote to that disappointment was his work. He'd thrown himself into his writing more than before, and the sales numbers and other rewards had kept him grounded.

His interest in Toni, however, was becoming more intense as the days went on, and he had to consciously rein himself in, both for his own sake and hers. The last thing he wanted was for her to feel overwhelmed in the face of his feelings for her.

And so he took his time with her. He had never felt so strongly and quickly about any other woman he'd known. As Hank got to know Toni better, he also realized that in addition to her drop-dead beauty, her sense of humor and playfulness made her a delightful companion. Her intelligence and compassion for others were added bonuses that he was discovering whenever they met. He couldn't believe his good fortune on the "night of the broken glass", as he fondly thought of that miraculous evening. He had brought her to his bed in a rush of instinct and love, not knowing what her response would be to his impetuousness. At that point in time, he didn't care. His normal patience and thoughtfulness could not control the speeding freight train of his need for her. He only knew that he had to be closer to her, had to make her feel his desire and his overwhelming sense of the rightness of their being connected both physically and emotionally.

Toni's response to his lovemaking was more than he could have hoped. Not only did she participate fully, but she seemed totally surprised and almost awe-struck by her response to him. When they rested for a while, her head on his chest, both feeling physically and emotionally spent, she began to cry.

Hank tilted her chin so that he could see her face and said, "What's wrong, lovey? Did I do something wrong? I thought you were enjoying everything."

She wiped away her tears and replied, "I've never felt anything like this in my life, Hank. I had no idea that what we did was even possible. I feel like there is a whole world here that I had no idea existed before tonight." As she said those last words, her right hand crept down between their bodies and cupped the bulk of him gently. Hank turned their bodies so that she was directly under his. As he slid down the length of her and rested for a moment between her knees, he looked up at her beloved face and said, "And I fully intend to introduce you to much more, my love."

In the pale light of the morning after, however, Toni had seemed to close her body and her heart to him. She was distant, preoccupied. Hank, both concerned and confused, asked her if there was something he'd done to disturb what to him had been the most wondrous lovemaking of his life. He quickly reviewed what they'd done and said all night and couldn't understand where he'd gone wrong. She set him straight, letting him know that it was she, not he, who was the problem.

She reassured him that his original assessment was mutual,

welcome news to Hank indeed, but that she was unprepared for the enormity of her feelings in the face of what had gone before in her life. She asked him, pleaded with him, to wait for her.

Hank reassured her that he would wait as long as she needed him to do so, vowing to himself that he would gladly take apart whoever had injured Toni so badly.

Chapter 15

Toni was so exhausted from the events of the previous few days that it was mid-morning when she woke up. She rolled over, looked at her clock on the bedside table and was amazed to find it was ten a.m.

Humphrey, sitting beside her, was calmly licking the fur on his chest, stealing glances at her to see if she was awake. "Hey, Humph, why didn't you wake me up? The day's partly gone; you must be hungry and so am I. Coffee first, then we'll plan what's left of the rest of the day." I'm getting to be as batty as some of my clients, she thought. Next thing, I'll be mumbling to myself as I walk into town.

She tied on her old chenille robe, slid into her favorite moccasins, and made her weekend coffee, a special blend of Starbuck's dark French roast and her regular ground coffee from Zehr's. To make it perfect, while the coffee was dripping, she pulled out a carton of table cream from the back of the fridge, squinted at the best-before date, and smiled. Small treats, she thought. She opened a can of Fancy Feast for Humphrey, who gave an imperious meow at the sound of the can opener. She watched him scarf up the concoction and then she headed into the living room to open her front curtains.

As she turned to go back into the kitchen, she saw an envelope on the floor in front of the door that led to the hallway that she shared with Hank. She picked it up and headed back to the kitchen. She poured her coffee and sat in her rocking chair, staring at her name on the front of the envelope in Hank's distinctive handwriting.

Open it, she told herself. What if it's bad news? What kind of bad news could it be, really, Antonia? Her alter ego was sounding annoyed. All right, she retorted, but I am worried, nonetheless. She opened the envelope, drew out the single piece of paper. Hank's words came into focus.

'Dearest Toni,

I'm off for a few days to a book signing, etcetera, arranged by my wonderfully exasperating agent, Stella. She KNOWS how much I hate these things, so she comes on like my mom and makes me feel guilty if I say no. Which is what I want to say, of course. Coincidentally, one of my stops is in Athabasca, would you believe? Would you like me to do some covert snooping, if I have time? I'd love to get the goods on you-know-who! I'll call you in a couple of days, before we reach Alberta.

Miss you. Remember I love you, Hank.'

She felt tears sliding down her cheeks when she read the ending. How she missed him, too. And how she wished her insecurities would take a long hike off a short bridge! What exactly did he mean by "etcetera"? Was he on some sort of holiday? And who was his beautiful dinner date the other night? God, she was gorgeous. Toni kept seeing Hank pull the woman into his arms on the front porch. Stop, you dopey girl, she thought.

She smiled at the thought of Hank "covertly snooping" in Athabasca, attempting to get information about James. It might be a good idea, though. He'd have to work his way into the English department on some pretext or other. That shouldn't be too hard for a well-known author, even if his books were meant for children. Maybe he could dig up some information that would give her some insight into why James was back in Guelph, pursuing her, his ex-wife.

She took a quick shower, dressed in her old, worn jeans, the ones with a hole in the right knee, a t-shirt and a plaid flannel jacket that she and Hank shared when one of them went outside to the garden. Before putting the jacket on, she held the collar up to her nose to see if his distinctive aroma was still on it. It never failed to make her smile: a combination of Irish Spring soap and pure male. Not like any other odor in the world, she thought.

She let herself into the back yard through the basement, Humphrey trotting along behind her, tail held high. She began raking the perennial beds along the back fence, the cat sunning himself on a nearby flat rock.

When she had moved into this wonderful house, she was not in the best emotional shape. Still entangled in the legal fallout from her divorce, she'd barely noticed Hank, or any other man, for that matter. She would find herself muttering "never again, never again" at odd times.

One evening a few weeks ago, Hank had asked her to go for a beer at the Woolwich Arms. She surprised both of them by accepting. They walked to the pub in the old house at the corner of Yarmouth and Woolwich Streets and ordered two drafts. They talked, and talked, getting to know each other better. After an hour or so, Hank got up to order a single malt for himself and a glass of white wine for Toni. As he stood at the bar waiting for the drinks, she looked over and was struck by his masculine good looks. She'd not noticed before now. Then she realized that looks aside, it was the sheer force of his personality that was so attractive. He made her feel like she was the only person in his world that mattered, her opinions, her feelings. His way of asking questions, combined with a curious, almost thirsty intellect, would be lethal, she thought, if she were available. But, of course, I'm not, available, that is.

A few more pub dates, dinner out, then dinner at his apartment, proved to her uptight mind that maybe she was available. It happened over a broken glass of Australian cabernet sauvignon. She stopped her raking and sat down next to Humphrey, who pushed his head into her hand while she remembered that miraculous evening.

His apartment was very different from what she'd expected, although, knowing Hank better at this point, she should have been prepared. He was a collector of early Canadiana, particularly stoneware jugs, and they were all over his rooms, on tables, tucked into corners, even in his bathroom. The rooms were also filled with antique furniture in original paint, and books. So many books – she'd never seen so many books in one place, outside of a library. He'd had to remove a stack of them from a chair so that she could sit at his dining room table. Papers covered the surfaces not taken up by jugs and books. The apartment seemed clean but to her untutored eye, messy.

He saw her looking at the piles of books and papers and said, "I know, it drives Mrs. Edwards, my cleaning lady, nuts. She's under strict orders to rearrange nothing, ever. She tried to reform me a long time ago, to no avail. She seems content, now, with muttered imprecations under her breath while she cleans around all the stuff. It may look like chaos, but it's my chaos and I know exactly where everything is."

Intractability aside, dinner was wonderful. He'd sautéed fresh swordfish in butter, with new boiled potatoes and parsley and sliced tomatoes dressed with a balsamic vinaigrette. After dinner, they sat on his soft leather couch, listening to Keith Jarret, sipping the last of their wine.

Hank took her hand in both of his, just as she reached for her glass on the coffee table. The glass broke into shards all over the floor. "Stay put, Toni. I'll clean it up." He left the room to get cleaning stuff. Toni reached down to pick up some of the bigger pieces of glass and promptly cut the palm of her left hand.

When Hank returned with cloths and vacuum, she tried to hide her hand, but he saw the blood seeping onto the floor. He pulled her injured hand onto his chest.

She could feel the strong rhythm of his beating heart. He picked her up off the couch and carried her into the bathroom. She looked down at his bloodied shirt and said, "I'll wash your shirt for you."

Hank sat her on the toilet seat while he washed and bandaged her hand, tenderly. "It's just a shirt, sweetheart. It can be replaced. You can't." And with that he picked her up again and brought her to his bed.

She still blushed when she remembered that night.

James had been a complete narcissist both in bed and out. It had never occurred to him that Toni's feelings might be of some importance when they made love. To James, the quantity of sexual acts seemed to matter more than the quality. One weekend, in the early days of their relationship, she had counted the number of times they'd connected sexually: eleven. The time period for each of those encounters was very brief; a few minutes of athleticism that always ended with James' shout of pleasure, followed by a hasty uncoupling that found them far apart on the bed. And, in retrospect, the satisfaction was all James', not hers. When she suggested that there were things that he could do to enhance her pleasure, he dismissed her words, saying, "Real women don't need any help." Needless to say, Toni didn't ask again.

That night with Hank obliterated any memories of James. Or the rest of the world, for that matter. When they paused for a while to sleep, Toni was astounded at how he still held her, cradling her head against his chest, his other arm firmly over her hip, drawing her to him. She woke at one point and realized that she couldn't tell where she ended and he began. They seemed fused, all tactile sense upended. She'd had no idea that it was possible to meld one's being into another's. When they made love that night and into the gray light of dawn, he made her feel that she was not only the most special person in the world but the only one.

Reality, of course, set in. Toni was so astounded by what Hank had shown her about herself that night that she grew afraid. Fearful of her response to him, of being so vulnerable that she could be hurt again. Her behavior after that night was to pull away from Hank and back into herself. He seemed to understand, but she wondered. They had connected again, a few weeks ago, but her response was the same the next morning. Would her damaged self ever recover, she wondered?

Chapter 16

Once the pile of leaves was raked from the perennial beds, Toni added them to the "pile of ruins" (Hank's and her term for the mound behind the garage). She and Humphrey headed back into the house for a cup of tea. Rather, Toni had the Earl Grey and Humph hunkered down over a saucer of kitty milk.

The phone rang. It was her brother, Fred. He sounded upset, agitated.

Toni, alarmed by her brother's distress, sank into her rocker, brushing stray curls from her face. "What's happening, Freddo?"

"I'm not sure where to start, Toni. Everything is even worse than before. I came home from work at suppertime tonight and found a note from Laura on the kitchen table. She's taken Georgie and the baby to her mother's and says that none of us will ever see my kids again. I don't know what to do..." His voice broke and a sob escaped.

Toni rose from her chair, her tea forgotten, and took a glass down from the cupboard and filled the glass with tap water. "Fred, talk to me. What led up to this? You seemed okay at Giuli's party..." She drank some water while she waited for her brother's reply.

"I thought things were okay, too, Toni. Laura had a really hard time after Peony was born, as you know. No colic this time, but the baby had taken a long time to settle into any kind of a routine, and Georgie was showing classic signs of jealousy. Temper tantrums, unwillingness to listen to our requests for him to follow his usual routines, talking back, etcetera. Given Laura's level of exhaustion, it was little wonder that her patience with Georgie was thin. I caught her spanking him over a matter that wouldn't have caused any punishment in the past. When I asked her about it, she was indignant and lashed out at me, blaming me for everything that was wrong in her life. And I know that she's been drinking again, even when her mother's not here. Our mom has expressed concern, doesn't know what to do, either. And to top it all off, I received a restraining order that will put me in jail if I try to see my kids."

Toni heard the desolation in his voice. She waited for him to continue.

"Help me, Toni – I am terrified that she will do something truly awful. I need to get my kids back, to know that they are safe, hold them in my arms again."

Toni heard the desperation in her brother's voice. Something dark, feral, rose up in her. She fought to keep those feelings at bay, knowing they would not help her brother. What she said instead was, "I will make some calls, Fred. We need to get all the help we can to make sure nothing harms your babies and that they are safely at home with you as soon as possible. I will get back to you as fast as I can, I promise. Get yourself something to eat while I see what I can do."

She sat in her chair, Humphrey curled up in her lap, her mind full of conflicting ideas and feelings. She had always had doubts about Laura but had kept them to herself, hoping that her misgivings were incorrect. 'Trust your intuition, Toni,' her inner voice prodded, once again. But, really, what could she have done, given Fred's determination and level of infatuation with his bride-to-be? People needed to make their own mistakes in order to find better paths for themselves, as she well knew. She just hoped that this mistake wasn't as colossal as it appeared.

She opened the drawer to her small telephone desk and leafed through her address book until she found the name she wanted. She dialed the number.

"Hello, Gloria, it's Toni Rossi here. Any chance of speaking to him?" She waited impatiently, her hand gripping the receiver. The avuncular voice sounded in her ear.

"Toni? How are you, my dear?" Her lawyer's tone, full of welcoming humor and concern, caused her emotions to calm. She tried for some levity as she assured him that she was fine but that she was reaching out to him on behalf of her brother.

Lawrence Winthrop had been one of the mainstays in Toni's divorce proceedings against James. He was a large, overweight bear of a man; however, his eating habits and lack of athleticism belied a whip-smart intellect and an ability to calm the most anxious of his clients. He had advised her, guided her and reassured her at every step of her journey away from her marriage to James. She had often thought that without Larry in her orbit at that time in her life, she might not have survived nearly as well as she had. She owed him more than she could hope to repay and had availed herself of his wisdom on more than one occasion afterward.

She filled in the information about Fred and his situation as briefly as possible. "I need to give him some reassurance, Larry, that there is some hope at the end of what could be a very long, painful tunnel."

His initial reply was not very reassuring. "I'm afraid that the response I have is not what you or your brother will be eager to hear, Toni." She could hear him clearing his voice as he tamped down what she knew was his pipe. The ritual of his pipe-fixing always gave him time to gather his thoughts. She waited.

"I have long seen this type of situation as a growing problem in the past few years. My colleagues, unfortunately, do not want to even discuss it, probably for fear of being seen as anti-feminist. To me, and I say this with great reluctance, it is the flip side of feminism. The legal and police professions seem to have gone way past the middle road here and are most often siding with and protecting women, regardless of the actual situation. Many men, as a result, are being victimized and worse, simply because they are men. I have tried for years to get people to recognize this as a growing problem, to no avail. It sounds as though your brother has landed in the middle of such a situation. And, in order to extricate him and his children, we will need to mount an air-tight defense and counter-offense that will be neither easy nor pretty. To say nothing of expensive. Is he up to being a part of this, Toni?"

"I'm sure he is, Larry. His children are his life. I know he will do whatever he needs to win them back and give them the kind of future they deserve. I will have him call you."

Chapter 17

Toni's thoughts turned to Bruce, and she again wondered where all that anger on Saturday morning had come from. Because of their long friendship and professional association, she knew he could be quick to anger, but he'd never turned on her before. Not like what happened the other day. It was very unnerving.

They were in the School of Social Work together at Wilfrid Laurier University and had become good friends, including Toni's friendship with Viv, Bruce's wife.

James had made it clear that both Bruce and Viv were beneath his notice ("not my type") when Toni asked why he was so cold toward them. James ascribed to the Machiavellian credo that only one percent of the population got things done. He, naturally, was in that small percentage of worthies. The remaining ninety-nine percent, whom he characterized as 'drones', did not deserve or receive his attention. Toni had ignored him and continued her friendship with the Pattersons.

Toni had been aware of Bruce's problems when they were graduate students together. Because of their training and extensive readings, she was sensitive to Bruce's tendencies fairly soon in their friendship. However, as she explained to one of her colleagues, she was also impressed by the extent of his knowledge and commitment to helping others less fortunate than himself.

Toni had said to her friend, "I often speculate that it might be because of his borderline issues that he is so eager to help those in need. He often rushes in when others express doubt about their ability to help. He has a real knack for forming tight friendships with some clients that other therapists might write off as 'hopeless'. In some situations, those friendships are lifelines to clients with no other resources. If only from that perspective," Toni had explained, "Bruce will be a beneficial partner to me."

Degrees in hand, Toni and Bruce had decided to set up their respective practices together. The old building at the corner of Woolwich and McTague was in the process of being renovated into professional office space, and they both knew it would be perfect for them. They could be close enough (Toni on the ground floor, Bruce on the second) for collaboration and consultation when required but not so close that either would feel hampered by too much proximity. They painted and furnished their own offices and hired the dependable Roxie to act as secretary, receptionist and general factotum for them and the other professionals in the building. They helped each other move in, pooled clients, held supervision meetings each week and remained good friends throughout.

Their venture had worked, and worked well, until now. Bruce seems to have come unhinged, she thought. "Great clinical diagnosis, Toni! Is a saner person 'hinged'?" Okay, knock it off, she told herself. You know darn well that he suffers from a borderline personality. You've seen it often enough with your own clients. They tend to form symbiotic relationships with people, any people. It matters not who the host is, as long as he or she is willing to carry the other for a while. And is willing to allow that person to feed off him or her emotionally.

Another characteristic of borderlines is their intense need for exclusivity in their relationship with the host. Wives are forbidden contact with their friends and families, and in extreme cases are kept almost prisoners in their homes.

Viv had committed the cardinal sin of rejecting Bruce. Not only had she turfed Bruce out of their home and marriage but had also rebuffed him in favor of another man, Max. No wonder Bruce's behavior was affected. All of the underpinnings of his life were gone. And, in the all-or-nothing thinking (feeling) of borderlines, he might as well die, because without Viv in his life, there was no hope. Nothing but a black void.

Toni knew that borderlines were prone to suicidal gestures, but most of these were attention-getting behaviors, as in "See how important I am to you?" Occasionally, however, the gesture became final when no one rescued the "poor victim" in time. Toni had seen the series of faint scars on the underside of Bruce's wrists and knew they were adolescent cries for help.

She was also aware of the borderline's apparent lack of personal boundaries when sexual behaviors were in play. Bruce had confided that he really enjoyed situations in which a woman had a young daughter that could be a part of his sexual advances as well.

Toni had recoiled in horror. She'd fought down her revulsion and said, "Bruce, I think you need to talk to someone about this type of activity."

"Why?" He'd seemed genuinely puzzled.

Holy God, she'd thought, he really has no understanding of the immorality of his behaviors, to say nothing of the legal consequences. She tried to make him realize the gravity of what he'd told her, to no avail. He didn't see his behavior as being abnormal at all. Viv had confided earlier that Bruce was very judgmental when it came to others' behaviors. The old saying, "Do what I say, not what I do" in practice.

Now Toni suddenly remembered Bruce's neglected cat and

hoped it was all right. How could he forget it?

She fed Humphrey, changed into slacks and a clean sweater, grabbed her corduroy jacket from the front closet and headed to meet Viv for dinner. She started toward her car then decided that since it was such a beautiful night, she would walk the few blocks to the Woolwich Arms pub.

Viv seemed really happy to see her friend. Her face was flushed, as though she'd had a head start on drinks before Toni's arrival.

"Viv – let's order some food to go with our drinks, okay?" She gestured toward the two empty glasses of margaritas lined up in front of Viv. Viv agreed and picked at her food when it arrived. She told Toni that Bruce had moved back in, temporarily, of course, just until he "got his bearings". She told Toni about this with a sheepish grin on her face.

Toni, surprised at this turn of events, asked her friend why this had happened.

She privately thought that Viv was enabling Bruce to continue with his self-destructive behavior. "If the truth be told," Viv said, "I don't want him, but I don't want anyone else to have him, either." Viv sighed, looking very sorry for herself.

Toni remembered Bruce's anger when he found out about Viv and Max. More precisely, when he found out that it was "his" money that was helping pay for the motels at which his wife and lover were rendezvousing. Never mind the fact that Viv, a secondary school teacher, earned as much income as Bruce and contributed equally to their living expenses. And that the "rendezvousing" occurred well after she and Bruce had separated.

"Sweetie," Toni leaned forward and grabbed Viv's hands in her own. "You need to wean yourselves away from each other.

Maybe cold turkey is asking too much right now, but Bruce needs to learn how to cope without you, at least for small periods of time. He also needs to see a clinician as soon as possible, and I know a good one. He's a really renowned therapist at the U, and I think he and Bruce would be a good fit." And, but she didn't say, Bruce has a history of violence that will probably be directed at his wife, Viv, in the near future. Toni wanted to get Bruce away from Viv as quickly as possible.

Viv expressed some reluctance, but said she'd think about it. Before Toni began walking home, she called a cab for Viv and made sure her friend was safely inside the vehicle.

The night was cool, a hint of frost in the air. Toni walked along Suffolk Street, thinking that she could feel the imminent start of winter. The sky was bright with stars, and fallen leaves crunched under her feet as she walked. Many of the old houses had windows filled with warm lights. Some were strung with Hallowe'en decorations. As she turned onto Glasgow, she was startled by a skeleton hanging from a tree. These things are getting more realistic-looking all the time; better be more careful, she thought.

She became aware of a barely audible car engine somewhere behind her. It was so quiet that she wasn't certain she'd heard it. When she turned to look behind her, she couldn't see anything suspicious. Just the usual row of cars parked on the right side of the street, where she was walking toward her house. Nothing out of the ordinary. There were no street lights on that section, so it was difficult to see much of anything. Houses were very close together and any light from the moon would be blocked by their height and breadth. Stop it, Toni, she admonished herself, only a little way to go.

She hurried along, trying not to break into a run. Her

instincts were telling her that something was wrong and that she needed to get away from some danger.

She could still hear an engine idling. She finally reached the sidewalk section opposite her house. All she had to do was look both ways and cross the street. As she stepped out from between two parked cars, she heard a car race toward her. It came so close to her that the wind created by the car's speed seemed to push her against one of the cars behind her. The speeding car's exhaust fumes were overwhelming. The car screamed around the corner at London Road and was gone.

Chapter 18

Toni hurriedly put on what she hoped was appropriate clothing for her role as guest speaker that evening at the Italian Canadian Club in The Ward district of Guelph. Mrs. Rossi and some of her friends were being honored by the club for their important roles in its development and growth through the years. This evening was a wonderful tribute to Angela Rossi and the small group of Italian immigrant women who were responsible for what the ICC had become today.

She heard Hank coming down the stairs and, after a last glance in the hall mirror, opened the door and met him in the front vestibule. "*Moltissima bella*, lovey," he said as he looked at her. "Did I say it correctly?" he asked, a bit worried about his pronunciation.

"*Perfetto*," Toni answered, putting her arm through his as they stepped onto the front porch together.

"Good," Hank said. "It's one of the few phrases I managed to learn today while listening to 'Italian for Dummies'. I'm afraid that the rest of my conversation tonight will be in 'Inglese', sad to say."

"Not to worry," Toni said. "My mom and her group of ICC women have spent decades learning English as a second language. Most have had to become fluent in English to keep up with their Canadian-born children, working husbands and their own jobs when required. My siblings and I became bilingual from the beginning; we spoke Italian at home with our parents but English in school and everywhere else. My mom was the least bilingual member in our family – her interactions with English-speaking people were very limited in her early years in Canada.

"Having four children, a house and a husband who was working long hours building a new business in a strange country were more than enough challenges in the early years. It was only later on, when my siblings and I began school and her workload lessened a bit that she was able to reach out to other women in her community and form the friendships that have endured all these years. She did become more fluent in her new country's language, but her Italian accent and its linguistic rules are ingrained in her heart. They are her comfort zone, her way of keeping as much of her beloved home country as close as possible. And we all love her tenacious grip on all things *Italiano*. A trip to Italy is definitely in my future."

Hank pulled her to him briefly and said, "Maybe we can make that trip together some day, *cara*." Toni tried unsuccessfully to wipe the grin off her face.

Hank opened his car door for Toni, and she slipped into the seat, glancing through the folder of notes to make sure she hadn't forgotten anything. She was no stranger to public speaking, accustomed to speaking engagements for the Sexual Education Center at the University of Guelph and the odd tutorial about various topics in the field of social work both in the community and as a guest speaker for CFRU, the University's radio station.

However, tonight's engagement was, in Toni's mind, a very different task. Not only had she been asked to be one of the guest speakers at the ICC, but she had also been given the very pleasant duty of honoring her own mother and her mother's community accomplishments.

As she and Hank parked the car and began walking toward

the ICC building, she remarked on how packed the parking lot seemed to be. "I had no idea what a big event this would be," she said to Hank, feeling a bit anxious at the size of the crowd heading toward the building's entrance. "I hope my mama isn't completely intimidated by all these people." Hank guided her through the crowd to the front of the auditorium and her place as one of the speakers.

"I'm sure you and she will be terrific," he said. "I'll see you later," and he made his way to the available audience seats.

Toni listened to the accolades given to the ICC's founding members and the "special" speaker of the evening, Frank Hasenfratz, CEO of Linamar Corporation. Frank's laudatory remarks about the ICC and its importance to the community of Guelph were very well received. Toni stood and applauded with the rest of the audience.

The moderator leaned into the microphone and announced the next speaker. "I now have the honor of introducing many of you to the daughter of one of our founding members – Doctor Antonia Rossi." The audience erupted into more applause. Toni knew that her face was a brilliant shade of scarlet as she made her way up to the podium. She nervously adjusted the microphone to her level and began by saying how tremendously honored she was to be asked to speak.

"I am doubly honored in that I have been asked to speak about one of my most favorite topics in the world: my beloved mama. My only hope is that she doesn't faint away at the embarrassment of being the object of so much attention. Sorry, Mama!" The audience laughed in appreciation and understanding.

"My parents immigrated to Canada in order to make a better life for their young family. Giovanni Rossi, my Dad, knew that his ability to make a good living in Italy would be limited by both geography and economic hardship. Their small village, south of Naples, never fully recovered after World War Two, and prospects for success were limited. After much deliberation, he and his young bride, the beautiful Angela D'Abruzzi, made the momentous decision to transplant themselves and their two young daughters to Canada. Giovanni had a good friend, Roberto Gagni, who had made the decision to move to a strange-sounding place, Guelph, Ontario. His letters home, to Giovanni and his wife, were full of the opportunities that Giovanni knew would benefit him and his family.

"With some reluctance and not a few misgivings, Giovanni and his small family decided to follow Roberto to Canada. His friend had assured him, Giovanni, that opportunities were his for the taking. The town of Guelph was growing rapidly, in step with its own university, and construction work was plentiful.

"Roberto had met another recent immigrant, a young fellow from Hungary, who was in the process of building a small business next to his house on the northern outskirts of Guelph, in a small village called Ariss. Roberto said that this fellow, Frank, had all kinds of ideas for the future and that Giovanni could step right into a full-time job when he emigrated from Italy to Canada.

"And so the momentous decision was made and the family arrived in Guelph. Roberto had found a small bungalow in The Ward area of Guelph that the Rossi family could rent, and Giovanni and his small family settled in. Giovanni began working alongside his friend, Roberto, and, in spite of the enormous move for the family, prospered. Frank Hasenfratz did indeed have plans for the future, and Giovanni and Roberto were two of the beneficiaries of his visions. The Ariss plant became the first of many satellite workplaces for the company that became Linamar, named after Frank's two daughters, Linda and Nancy and his wife, Mary. The company went on to expand to Europe and beyond. In time, it became the largest employer in Guelph, only surpassed by the University of Guelph in its number of employees."

Toni paused for a sip of water. She noticed that some of the current Linamar employees in the audience were smiling in appreciation.

"Giovanni and Roberto formed their own incorporated construction business and, in time, in response to his own health problems, Roberto sold his shares of the company to Giovanni. Roberto was never far from Giovanni's thoughts, however, and Roberto was able to act as a mentor and sounding-board to Giovanni as the newly minted company, Rossi Construction Ltd., grew and prospered.

"Angela gave birth to Freddo and then me, Toni, in the years that followed the move to Canada. Our mama was more than content to raise their four children, keep house and tend to their enormous kitchen garden behind the bungalow on Alice Street in The Ward. She eventually developed friendships with a large group of other Italian immigrant wives, and these women and their families helped stave off Angela's home-sickness and any feelings of alienation that she felt at her family's arrival in Canada. Their common backgrounds and experiences were very instrumental in helping the Rossi family settle into their new country.

"After a few years of living in Guelph and watching her children prosper in school, Angela and a group of other immigrant Italian women decided that what their community needed was a common gathering place for birthdays, anniversaries and various interest groups. They envisioned a place where Italian immigrants could come together for meetings, clubs, and special events; where there was a large kitchen that they could prepare and share the Italian recipes they'd brought from 'home'. And so, the Italian–Canadian Club was conceived and built, east of Elizabeth Street in The Ward. In time, the building became a landmark not only in The Ward but also in the rest of Guelph and its surrounding areas. The club became self-supporting by renting the main hall and kitchens to various local groups, some Italian, some not. However, its original conception and intent remained, and the ICC in The Ward became a sought-after destination for various groups. Linamar Corporation, Giovanni's first Guelph employer, became one of its biggest supporters."

There was a smattering of applause as Toni turned over the page of her speech.

She smiled at some of the familiar faces near the front of the hall.

"We four Rossi children, first-generation immigrants for all practical purposes, were bilingual. Italian was spoken at home; English was learned and spoken in the school system and elsewhere. Because of her circumstances and limited opportunity to learn the English language, Angela was the least bilingual member of the Rossi family. Her husband became more fluent in English because of his work and the people with whom he interacted every day.

"My siblings and I took to our new country and language with ease. We would tease our mom about her unwillingness to follow in our footsteps with respect to our bilingual abilities. Her answer to our teasing was to reluctantly learn the necessities of the English language for shopping and other moments when Italian wouldn't suffice for communication. Otherwise, at home and with her large group of Italian friends, she did not see the necessity of learning English.

"My dad's company, Rossi Construction, grew and prospered. It became instrumental in the development and growth of not only Linamar and its many plants in the Guelph area but also the University of Guelph. The university had wisely bought and then leased hundreds of acres of land in the area south of the downtown core and beyond. And Freddo, his name now anglicized to Fred, continued the tradition begun many years ago by Giovanni and his good friend, Roberto.

"Rossi Construction Ltd. was known for its quality and good stewardship of not only its projects but also of its large workforce. Trade unions and memberships were encouraged. Employment, salaries and working conditions at Rossi were much sought after. Turnover was very small and job openings in the construction company scarce. Fred, knowing the importance of education, developed scholarships for his employees' children. He also brought in a daycare center for their children and an extensive benefits program that emphasized achievable retirement goals. In line with these goals, after the company was incorporated and listed on the Toronto Stock Exchange, he gave individual shares of the company to employees who met certain criteria. He knew, thanks to business courses at the university, that employees who held vested interests in their own company would be more willing to work hard in order to see their company thrive in a competitive workplace."

Again, more applause as Toni continued with her story. She said, "Not to worry, I'm almost done!" There was laughter from the audience.

"My mama continued her work with her friends, expanding the work and usefulness of their small group that made up the original core of the ICC. She has been particularly instrumental in the development and implementation of the ICC's outreach programs. These programs address issues such as poverty, homelessness and child mental health. I won't take time to enumerate all of her good work tonight. It speaks for itself. What I do want to say is that I am certain that without my mother and her friends, the Italian community in Guelph, and Guelph in general, would be sorely lacking in the type of warmth, good works and fabulous food we all know and love. And now, I would like to introduce my mama and her friends to all of you!"

The small group of friends stood up, accompanied by much applause, and reluctantly made their way up to the podium, where Toni stood, beaming. She embraced her mama and introduced the other women to the audience. The moderator brought out an embarrassingly large trophy, set it on a table beside the women and asked if any of them would like to say a few words. They huddled among themselves and whispered in Italian. Finally, one very nervous volunteer said a few words of thanks, after which she quickly stepped back into the group.

The moderator thanked Toni and the group of women and announced that refreshments would be served in the lobby.

Toni and Mrs. Rossi met up with the rest of the Rossi family, all of whom were giddy with relief and happiness that the formal ceremony was over. Mrs. Rossi hugged and thanked Toni over and over for her kind words. "You were *magnifico, Cara! Grazie tanto ancora et ancora.*" She thanked her daughter again and again, tears in her eyes.

Toni reassured her mom repeatedly that it was her great pleasure to give her speech and that she had been honored to be asked to do so. They made their way, slowly, to the lobby and welcome refreshments.

Toni looked for Hank and saw him across the room, in conversation with a tall, thin, aristocratic-looking man. When she realized who it was, she made quick excuses to her family and hurried over to where Hank was conversing with the man. As she approached them, she could tell that the tenor of the conversation was not very uplifting. She reached Hank's side, putting her left hand on his arm and holding out her right hand to her ex-husband.

"James, I had no idea you would be here this evening. How did you hear about this event?" She tried for levity and a positive tone, secretly seething inside. How dare he come to an event meant for her beloved family, knowing how disruptive his presence could be to them?

True to form, his response was haughty, entitled. "I saw the notice in *The Mercury* and thought that my presence might be welcomed. I have been disabused of that notion by your new 'friend'." He made the word "friend" sound like a bad word. Toni could feel Hank stiffen. She lightly squeezed his arm, attempting to forestall any further unpleasantness.

Unwilling to prolong or provoke the interaction between the two men, Toni thanked James for coming, saying that she would convey his good wishes to her mother, and led Hank off toward the refreshments table. She hoped that her abrupt leave-taking would be hint enough that any further contact from James would be unwelcome to her and her family. She glanced back and saw with relief that James was making his way to the exit. His scowl was noticeable.

Hank put his arm around Toni and thanked her for rescuing him. "I was worried that we would come to blows, verbal or otherwise. Thank you for forestalling whatever might have happened. I mean it!" He kissed her cheek.

"We'll talk about it later," Toni said. "I'm sorry that you met

James without me there. This evening is for my mama. Let's find her and the family. And try to put that encounter out of our minds for a while." Hank agreed, and they went off to find the rest of the Rossis.

When they were back in Hank's apartment, Toni brought up the subject of James and his unexpected appearance. "Tell me what happened, please." They were sitting close together on the couch, sipping glasses of pinot grigio.

Hank told her that after the ceremony, he slipped out into the lobby in search of the men's room. As he washed his hands at the sink, he glanced at the man next to him, who was staring at him in the mirror. Hank asked if he knew him, and the man introduced himself as James Barrington the Third, former husband of Antonia Rossi. Hank said he made his name sound like minor royalty. And not in a good way, he added.

The two left the washroom at the same time, and James indicated that he wanted to speak to Hank privately. Hank, wary but curious, agreed, and the two found a corner in the lobby where they could talk.

When Hank asked why James had come to the awards ceremony, James said that he still considered himself a part of the Rossi family but said it as though they should be grateful that he had bothered to attend, implying that his time would have been better spent in more worth-while endeavors. Hank, bristling on behalf of Toni and her family, was in the process of tearing a strip off James and his superior attitude when Toni appeared.

"It was good that you rescued me when you did, lovey. I've never punched anyone, but I must admit that I was ready to haul off and belt this guy, as they say. And damn the consequences. Enough said. I'm sorry that he provoked such a reaction in me. How could you tolerate him?" He said the last words in perplexed wonder.

She looked at Hank over her wine glass and said, "I couldn't, finally. When we first met, I was very young and inexperienced and the fact that a well-known professor was interested in me was mesmerizing. However, through the years of our marriage, that attitude of superiority was part of what unraveled my feelings for him, in addition to other awful behaviors. I stopped believing in him and saw him for what he really was. I understand that his attitude is a cover-up for deep insecurity, but I had neither the time nor the willingness to uncover the many layers of defense that he'd built up during his life. Leaving, as difficult as it was, was my only recourse. I'm glad, strange as it may sound, that you saw him as he is. I hope that that encounter doesn't happen again."

She saw the love and understanding in his eyes and felt it in the warmth of his long hug. He put down his glass and said, as he pulled her to her feet, "Come."

Chapter 19

"John, let's talk about what you would like to happen in your marriage the second time around." John sat in his chair, a puzzled look on his face, as if his therapist had just asked him to develop a new algorithm.

God, thought Toni. It's like pulling teeth. The funny thing was that this estranged couple actually seemed to have a chance at reconciliation. If only she could get them to talk to each other.

She tried another tactic. "Kim, while John is thinking about some answers to my question, why don't you let him know what you would like to happen. And then let's see if there are any similarities between what each of you wants." Kim, less stolid and infinitely more communicative than her nonverbal husband, took out a written list from her purse and began reading to John.

Well, Toni mused, at least someone is prepared here. While Kim talked, Toni thought about Bruce and Viv. She was concerned about the escalation of violence that Bruce was showing. And about Viv's lack of concern in the face of Bruce's behavior. Toni knew that Viv was exhibiting signs of enabling Bruce's condition. She knew that she'd have to talk to Viv about her suspicions, as soon as possible.

She also realized that a therapist other than herself would need to handle the situation with her friends. Someone with no emotional involvement with the couple was required here. She knew someone at the University of Guelph who might be a good fit with Bruce.

"So what do you think, Dr. Rossi?" Toni forced her attention back to the present and turned the question around. "Let's find out how John feels about what you just said."

After her last client left, Toni stopped at the receptionist's desk to say goodnight to Roxie. "Has Dr. Patterson been in today?" Roxie reminded Toni that he had canceled his appointments for this week. Something about meetings in Toronto.

He said he'd be checking in each day by phone but so far hadn't called. Toni, trying to reassure Roxie after Bruce's bizarre behavior Saturday morning, said she was certain he'd check in tomorrow.

She drove to her parents' house. She'd made arrangements earlier in the day with her mom, saying that she needed to discuss something with them. Her mother insisted her daughter come for dinner.

"*Carissima*," her papa bellowed, seeing her walk up the driveway toward his vegetable gardens. "*Come stai?*" His hug was huge and enveloping. "You look like you could use some food, *bella*. You mama she make lasagna, *insalata* and your favorite dessert, *panfrutto*." Her parents knew Toni's weakness for her mother's plum cake.

"Papa, if you had your way I'd be as big as a house," Toni teased. It was an on-going skirmish since Toni had lost her teenage chubbiness, moved away to university and beyond. She appreciated her parents' concern for their slender daughter, who had no intention of reverting back to her childhood eating habits, fueled by her mother's amazing meals. "How's the garden doing, Papa?"

"Good, good. Lot of rain, lot of summer sun. Everything *tutto bene*. All's left is carrots, parsnips and horseradish. Then I put to bed for winter." Her dad's homemade horseradish was enough to reduce most hot spice lovers to gasps for water. Tears had poured down James' face after his first taste. He'd been full of bravado prior to the meal, protesting that nothing could be that hot. She smiled at the memory of James' quiet fury. Hot horseradish: how to reduce anyone to a common denominator, came the unbidden, smug thought.

Toni headed for the kitchen through the back door and mud room. The aromas were wonderful, beckoning and embracing, just as her mama did when her daughter came into the kitchen. "*Ciao*, Mama," Toni said, feelings of love and security overwhelming her as usual, in her mother's hug. Her mama's face was flushed, gray hair in an untidy bun, tendrils sticking to her cheeks.

"*Bambina*. So good to see you again, so soon. Take your coat off and I pour you a glass of wine. Sit, sit…"

Although Toni had never lived in the house on Grange Street, she had loved the feel of the house as soon as her parents moved in. The house seemed to offer the unconditional love and acceptance all children need. And many never find. She told herself once more how fortunate she was to be born into this family.

She recounted a mild version of Bruce and Viv's problems to her parents during dinner. She left out the incident with the car from the night before and the worst of Bruce's violent behavior. No need to worry her parents unnecessarily. She often thought that if they weren't Italian, they'd make great Jewish parents.

Hank said that his mother, gone for many years, would call him daily to remind him to eat, get enough rest, etcetera. He said it used to drive him slightly crazy. Now, of course, he'd give anything to have her nagging at him again.

Her mama was philosophical about Toni's friends' marital problems. "Marriage is hard work, Antonia. Some people don' like to put out much effort. It's not just about love. Sometimes you have to give when you don' want to, compromise on things that are important and do some things that you think are not gonna be doable. You papa and I have had some not so good times, but somehow, we knew we'd get through, and always together. We are best friends for each other. We lean on each other, but never too much. Never too much." She gazed with adoration at her embarrassed husband. She then pinched Toni's cheek and smoothed back her daughter's unruly curls. "You learn as you go, c*ara*, always with love."

Her mother asked about Hank. Her parents were aware of the feelings between him and their daughter.

"He's away on a book tour right now, Mama. He will call me tonight."

"Such a nice man, Toni. If only he were *Cattolico*..." Her mother's voice trailed off as she turned toward the sink with an armload of dishes.

Toni's eyes rolled up to the ceiling as she answered, "Mama, if Hank's mother were alive, she'd be saying the same things about me. 'So why a shiksa, Hankeleh? A nice Jewish girl wouldn't do?' The last time I checked, Mama, the heart didn't have a brain. The world would be a very different place if it did."

As her mother served coffee, Toni asked her parents what had happened when they had met James at Tim Horton's on Saturday morning. Her mother answered. "It was kinda strange, *cara*. We park the car and walk toward the donut shop's entrance. A car was park nearby, its engine running. I no see person in car. It seem like he was waiting for someone, yes? We go in store, you papa order, we sit down, and all a sudden James stands in doorway, lookin' at us. We invite him over, of course. We have little Giuli with us, James make big fuss over her.

"Almos' like he try to get on our good side? Giuli tol' him

about her party and invite him to come before we realize what happen'."

"I no like him, *cara*," Toni's dad interjected. "Up to no good. Shoulda' stayed in Uppa Canada – good place for his kind." Her dad stirred his coffee, clearly embarrassed at his outburst. Her Dad's use of the term "Upper Canada" wasn't accurate, but Toni knew what he was trying to say.

"I'm so sorry that he bothered you, Mama, Papa. I had no idea that he was in Guelph until a few days ago. I'm not sure why he's here, but if I see him again, I'll tell him not to bother you any more."

Mrs. Rossi said, "Don't worry about us, *bambina*. Jus' don' let him convince you to take him back, or somethin'. You dad is right. Somethin' not right… Was almos' like he want somethin' from us. Especially from Giuliana. I no like him." She hit the tabletop with her open palm. The smack reverberated in the cups and saucers, spilling some of the espresso.

The conversation turned toward other topics. Toni leaned across the table and took her mother's hands in her own. "Mama, Papa, I have some other news that I need to talk to you about." Her parents, hearing and seeing the seriousness in her voice and face, sat still.

"You know that Freddo has been having some trouble at home, what with the new baby and all, and Laura's struggle managing both Georgie and the inevitable sleepless nights. Fred told me that Laura has taken the kids to her mother's house and is telling Fred that he can't see his babies." She waited for her parents' reaction to this devastating news.

"What? Not see his *bambinos*? What kind of thing is that, Toni?" Her mother looked horrified, her father equally as shocked.

"What can this mean?" he asked his daughter.

Toni explained what Fred had told her as clearly as she could. Her parents, stunned by this news, asked if that meant they couldn't see their grandchildren, too. Toni allowed that that was probably the case. In an attempt to lessen the blow, she explained that Fred would be talking to the same lawyer that Toni had used for her divorce. She was sure that it would be a while before her parents would be able to process this terrible news. She promised that as soon as she had any information she would be in touch with them.

She felt terrible leaving them but knew that they would deal with this as they dealt with other bad news, together. They would talk, discuss, remonstrate, do whatever needed to be done to process this awful information, and, as usual, move forward together. A supportive bulwark against life's bad news. She envied them their ability to weather life's tragedies this way and marveled at the strength and certitude their relationship gave them. She knew that at the end of the process, their front would be united and full of compassion for Fred and his babies.

Toni drove home and as she opened the door, the phone rang. She hurried toward the phone and grinned when she heard Hank's voice. "Where are you, Hank? You sound like you are in the next room."

"Would that I were, lovey. I'm lying on the bed in a hotel room in Saskatoon, in the altogether, thinking about you." His voice was a rough purr in her ears.

"Hank, my ears are burning!" She pretended shock.

"I'd be happy to set the rest of you on fire, too, sweetie. I miss you awfully."

"And I you," Toni said. She sketched an outline of the latest events. James' strange behavior, Fred's problems, the latest soap opera with Bruce and Viv, and the car on Glasgow Street last night. She tried to keep it as light-hearted as possible. She didn't succeed.

When she finished, Hank's voice sounded alarmed. "Did you call the police about the car? Christ, you could've been killed. What kind of bastard would do something like that? Could James be totally off his rocker? From what you've just told me, it might be possible."

Toni regretted telling him about the car. "It might have been a mistake, so I didn't call the police. Maybe the driver didn't see me and was just speeding up what he thought was an empty side street. I couldn't tell what kind of car it was or see the driver or the license plate." The more she tried to convince Hank of the nonseriousness of the event, the more she was convincing herself. "And I don't think James has a car, Hank. I drove him to his hotel the other night after dinner." She hadn't told Hank about the taxi waiting at the hotel. She was reluctant to alarm Hank any more than was necessary.

His alarm slightly mollified, Hank became urgently protective. "Promise that you won't walk alone at night, sweetie. If you do have to go out at night, have your cell phone in your hand and a can of mace in your pocket, both when you go to your car and when you leave it. How about staying at your parents' until I can get home?" He sounded really worried.

"I'm not scared, Hank. Honest. I'm not really worried about James, and the car incident was most likely a fluke." She tried to sound more confident than she felt. She didn't want Hank to spend his book tour time worrying about her instead of promoting his wonderful books. She also sketched in her conversation with Fred and her dinner with her parents. Hank expressed alarm at Laura's ultimatum to Fred and asked Toni to convey his support to her brother.

They talked about Hank's upcoming trip to Athabasca. Toni didn't know any of the faculty in the English department there. Hank said he'd do what he could without raising suspicions. He told her he'd phone each night to make sure she was safe and well. He reminded her again about not walking alone at night. Pleased with his concern, Toni was confident that he was overreacting.

Toni phoned Viv, hoping for some good news. "Toni – you'll never guess what Bruce did!" She sounded excited and happy. Toni waited. "He hired a decorator to re-do the small room off the kitchen for me."

Toni knew that Viv had been wanting to have her own office at home for some time. She'd been gathering paint chips and fabric samples for a while. The separation with Bruce had interfered with those plans.

"That's great, Viv. But what about the plans that you made?"

"Bruce says this woman is really good. I guess he's already told her what to do. He says I'll love it. Isn't it nice of him to do this?"

Toni could think of a lot of things this action of Bruce's was. Nice wasn't one of them. Controlling and manipulative would be more like it. Viv, as usual, had been charmed again by her husband and his needs.

"It's great," Toni said, not wanting to deflate Viv's good mood. "Have you given any more thought to the therapist I told you about? And did you mention him to Bruce?"

Viv sounded contrite. "I couldn't, Toni. He was in such a good mood when he was here. He really seemed better." Toni doubted that. Bruce could turn on the charm at will when he wanted something badly enough.

She reminded Viv about the scene Bruce had created at the office on Saturday morning. How he had lost control in front of Roxie and several clients, swore at Toni and yanked her hair. "That was only two days ago, Viv."

Silence on the other end of the phone. Then, "What can I say, Toni? You must have made Bruce mad."

Ouch, Toni thought. After a brief spasm of dismay at her friend's words, Toni realized that Viv was still protecting her ex, unable to see him clearly, denying the obvious problems. It would take time…

Chapter 20

Viv sank back into her headboard after her conversation with Toni. She ran her hand through her hair, thinking about what Toni had said, Bruce's behavior lately, and his determination to weave his way back into their life together, regardless of the separation that they had mutually agreed upon. No matter what she did to indicate that she wasn't going to allow him back in, he seemed to renew his efforts on a daily basis.

Viv had heard about abused women who were unable to leave their abusers.

She could never really understand how this could happen to someone who was the victim in a bad relationship. What would make a person continue to stay in such a situation? Now she was beginning to understand some of the reasons why this behavior existed. Part of it had to do with her guilt about leaving Bruce and wondering if she was making the right decision. She still had positive feelings for him, and he could be very persuasive when he sensed her indecision. Part of it was a worry about the unknown. At least she knew what to expect from Bruce.

What if she ended up in a worse situation? Maybe this was all she could hope for in a relationship. These thoughts and others like them had kept her from behaving differently for a long time. Her low self-esteem and fear of the unknown were powerful deterrents and had kept her from thinking about other possibilities.

However, she had gradually begun listening to what Toni

was saying to her. It had taken her time to really hear and absorb some of her friend's concerns. Her initial impulse had been to block out what Toni was saying, even though part of her knew that what Toni was saying was true.

She tried to explain her ambivalence to Toni. "I am torn between my lingering feelings for Bruce, Toni. It's hard not to remember the good times at the beginning of our relationship, even though what is happening now is so different. On the other hand, I see what is developing with Max and his treatment of me. It is so different from what I experienced with Bruce that I can't help but pay attention.

"Max's marriage has been coming apart for a while, and he and I often discuss what a future might look like for us together. We've resolved to take the smallest of baby steps with each other. We are not only determined to not make the same mistakes as before but to put in place new, more flexible standards that can accommodate our needs and allow each of us breathing room along the way."

When Viv found herself initially being pulled back by Bruce's needs and demands, she felt that she had somehow failed, again. And, sad to say, it was easier to acquiesce into the known than to move toward an unknown future. Guilt was also playing its role at being an added deterrent from moving forward.

As tempting as it was, however, moving backward was no longer an option. Viv had to do what was best for her own health and survival. She now knew that the way forward was something that required not only strength and resolve, but also that it was the only way to go.

Bruce's latest attempts at reconciliation included bringing her small gifts every day. If she wasn't home, he would leave a small bag on her back doorstep. Today's offering (as she thought of his presents) was a pair of earrings that he'd found at the local market in Guelph. When Bruce had begun these daily presents, she had tried to discourage him.

"Bruce, I appreciate your gifts to me, but they are not necessary, and I wish that you would stop bringing me things."

"But sweetie," he had replied, looking as sad as a hound dog whose owner had just chastised him for messing up a stack of pillows on the couch, "I want to bring presents to you. I really enjoy picking things out, thinking about how much you will enjoy them. It gives me so much happiness to be doing this for you."

Seeing the unnecessary hurt that she was inflicting on him, she backed off and didn't mention the presents again. They kept on coming, regardless of how she felt about his intentions. His attempts at bribery might be well meant, but they were a burden to Viv, good intentions or not.

Part of her felt sorry for him, but not sorry enough to let him into her life on a full-time basis. She knew that Toni was right in her assessment about the unhealthiness of their relationship and its effect on her, Viv. But sometimes she felt so guilty about not wanting to be with him any more that her defenses could be breached in a heartbeat. Especially when they'd been drinking together.

Bruce was very adept at arranging things so that a dinner together would turn into an evening of drinking a lot of wine. After a few hours of chardonnay, Viv's good intentions would be thrown out the window. The next rational thought would find Viv waking up in the morning, her head pounding and her bed in complete disarray. Often there would be a note on her nightstand, something to the effect that last night was terrific and "See you later on today, as agreed." Viv, disoriented and nauscous, would wonder about what the "agreement" could be. She knew that she'd be informed soon enough. Another of Bruce's latest habits, in addition to the unwanted gift-giving, was to phone her several times each day.

When she attempted to discourage these frequent phone calls, Bruce would pretend innocence. "But sweetie, I need to know that you are okay and that we can get together after work. How about dinner tonight?" Viv knew that his real motivation was to check up on her whereabouts and/or proximity to Max. And, in spite of her good intentions, she would give in to Bruce's needs and agree to his suggestions. Again.

Bruce regarded Max as his competition. He frequently asked Viv about Max and his habits, where they were going to dinner, etcetera. He even tried to get Viv to tell him how Max was in bed with her: did she like what he did, how long did the lovemaking last, did she have orgasms, etcetera. Viv, offended at these personal questions, refused to answer Bruce, and eventually the inquisitions stopped. However, Bruce was undaunted by Viv's relationship with Max. In fact, her being involved with Max had the effect on Bruce of a proverbial red flag to a bull. The longer the affair went on, and the more Viv was involved with Max, the more effort Bruce made to win back his bride.

Viv knew that the only way that she could make Bruce really understand that she would not be returning to their marriage was to cut her ties with him and not encourage him when she felt sorry or guilty about the change in her feelings toward him.

"It's so hard," she said to herself now. "We've been together for so many years, and I have some good memories of the early times, when it seemed to be Bruce and me against the world." She remembered a conversation they'd had a short while ago that had made Viv clearly see how far Bruce had gone into his borderline personality problems. They'd been reminiscing about when they first met and what each of them saw in the other person. Viv had told Bruce that his upbeat personality was one characteristic that she appreciated.

"A lot of the teachers that I socialized with were so serious and pragmatic, Bruce. You seemed to be so light-hearted and irreverent about the same issues. And it was like a breath of fresh air being in your company."

Bruce countered her compliments with a lengthy analysis of what he'd been looking for in a romantic partner. "I knew that I needed someone who could just be with me and only me. Someone who had few, if any, attachments to anyone else, who didn't want any rug-rats taking up her time and attention with me. You seemed like the perfect fit for what I wanted. I knew other women who might be suitable, but then I'd find out that they had big families and wanted to have lots of kids with me. I knew it wouldn't work with any of them."

Viv knew that the warning signs were there from the beginning, but she was too much in love to heed any of them. She had always thought she might want children of her own, but when Bruce made it clear that he just wanted it to be the two of them, she was secretly thrilled at his possessiveness. She now understood all too clearly what that possessiveness meant.

"Things have changed for me, Bruce. What we had at the beginning was what I thought I needed for the rest of my life. However, I have changed in what I want as I get older. I would really like to have children of my own and not only that, I need a relationship that can include other people and other points of view. One in which I have room to grow and change. And a life partner who is not worried about these changes either in me or in himself. I don't think that the static cocoon that you and I are in is healthy for me now." She said the last with some regret, as she really had thought in their early years together that exclusivity was the right way to be. Now she knew that Bruce's needs and problems had required her to put aside what was right and healthy for her.

Bruce, as usual, either didn't understand what Viv was trying to tell him or did understand and couldn't accept it. "I always thought we were on the same page together, honey. Why can't I be enough for you, the way I used to be?" The last was said in a whiny undertone.

Viv now knew that there had to be a complete severing of her contact with Bruce so that he would finally understand that the marriage was over. She just wasn't certain how to go about doing this or if she could do it. Maybe Bruce would find someone else to attach himself to, someone unsuspecting and more innocent and malleable than Viv was now. She wondered if the fantastic Sheila would be the one to turn Bruce's head. As she turned out the light, her last thought was that she would think about it again, tomorrow.

Chapter 21

I wonder if he has any idea how happy he makes me when he calls, Toni thought after her conversation with Hank. It makes all the other aspects of my life, especially the bad ones, bearable.

'He's not a mind-reader, chickie,' interjected her alter ego. 'If you don't tell him, he won't know what you're thinking.'

"I know, I know," Toni remonstrated, shaking her head. "It's hard for me to be that vulnerable with him, after all that's happened before I met him."

'So, you think you're the only one that's had it tough? Gonna be a lot harder if you lose him,' came the retort.

'Don't remind me,' she thought. 'I wish I'd had the courage to ask him who his beautiful date was the other night. Maybe it was one of his writer friends. Or someone from the publishing world. But they seemed sooo… friendly. Stop it!' Toni slapped the heel of her hand to her forehead. Such a *'pazza bambina'*, as her family would say.

Or Hank, in his deep rumble, "Get a grip, bubbie."

Her thoughts returned to James and when they had met. Toni was an undergraduate in one of James' English literature classes. She'd been in awe of him.

Viv had asked her why she was so attracted to James. Toni's answer was indicative of her age and inexperience. "He's very handsome, his long dark hair is pulled back in a ponytail, his eyes are bright, almost glittering when they focus on me in class, Viv. He seems to pull answers from me with his dark stare, his look penetrating, demanding. I want to be the best I can be for him. I find him so interesting and intelligent, and I try hard to give him the answers he's looking for. I want him to see that I am the smartest girl in his class and the one he should pay the most attention to."

Viv, worried about her friend's fascination for her older professor and his interpretation of her motives, tried to caution her friend.

"Be careful, Toni. You don't want him to get the wrong idea about your interest in him. Try to make it clear that your efforts are academic, not personal. Lesser men than he have fallen astray in the face of single-minded devotion. He's only a man, after all."

Toni heard what Viv was telling her and the wisdom her advice conveyed. However, her heart seemed determined to overrule her brain, and so the story continued to unfold as it would.

No matter what Toni did, it was never enough for her professor. She spent more time on his papers, answered more questions in class and studied harder for his exams than for her other elective classes. In spite of all her effort, she only managed to get a B plus. When she checked with fellow students, she found that most of their marks were even lower than hers. Some consolation.

When the school year was over, James asked her out on a date. As their relationship progressed, more slowly than Toni would have liked, she found herself obsessed, again, trying to win James' approval for what she was doing, who she was. He claimed to love her while at the same time never being really satisfied with her. She wasn't rational enough, thin enough, independent enough. Always a bridesmaid, Toni thought. Never a bride. Her friends weren't intellectual enough, and her family still bore the marks of recent Canadian immigrants. According to

James, this was some kind of personal defect on her parents' part.

She found herself jealous of women whom he openly admired, yet knew that she could never measure up to them. When he finally asked her to marry him, she had serious doubts and told him so.

His answer to her doubts was flattering. "I know that I need to work toward becoming a better person, Toni, and I also know that you can help me do this."

She was more than flattered; she was disarmed. He was admitting that he had problems while at the same time asking for her help with them. She was stunned that he would place his confidence in her ability to help him grow and change.

"And so, dear reader, they were married."

Her family and friends were openly opposed to the marriage and had tried without success to talk her out of it. Her mama, in particular. "*Bambina*," she said when Toni told her of her intentions, "are you sure he is the right man for you?"

Toni answered by asking her mom a question. "What makes you think he might not be, Mama?"

Her mom's answer was short and to the point. "He no seem to like you much, *cara.* I see how he look at you, not with *amore*, more like *dispiacere*. He no seem to like you much."

Toni, nonplussed by her mama's words, said, "Oh Mama, I think you don't know him very well. He tells me how much he loves me all the time." If she had been older and more experienced, she would have been able to pay attention to the warning signs. It was a while before she understood the disconnect between James' words and his behavior.

If he loved her, why was he so openly interested in other women? Why was he so contemptuous of her friends and family? And why did he attempt to push her into trying mind-altering drugs, wife-swapping, etcetera? Without success in the last two endeavors, thankfully, as she remembered his cajoling, her own shock. He'd eventually backed off in his attempts to convince her to "open up".

The day her love for him ran out was when she discovered that he'd had a one-night stand with his friend, Arnold. While trying to rein in her outrage, betrayal and disgust, she asked him why he had done this. James' response: "I mean to try everything life has to offer, at least once. I am sorry that you are upset," (Upset? she thought... That didn't begin to describe what she felt) "but if I had the chance, I'd do it again." The implication was that he felt no remorse for what he had done and was only sorry that she had reacted so negatively toward his behavior. It became apparent to Toni that his intentions of becoming a better person, with or without her help, were insincere. His behaviors became less defensible as time went on.

The final nail in the coffin of their marriage was hammered in when James was accused of sexual harassment by some students. The discovery that she, Toni, was pregnant with a severely damaged fetus was anticlimactic. He had tried to elicit a promise from her that she would keep the baby, in spite of the medical advice they'd received.

"I can't believe that you would want to have an abortion, Toni. Killing our child would be a sin. Surely you understand that." Toni said she'd think about what he was saying, all the while reeling with the collapse of their marriage and the accusations of the university.

After she had the abortion, she told James what she had done. His fury was palpable. He said, "Mark my words, Toni. I will make sure that you regret your unforgivable behavior."

He removed himself to Athabasca and a much less

distinguished position at their university. The next time she saw him was three years later in her kitchen, this past week.

His attitude toward her seemed different now. He seemed to be seeking her approval, somehow. As if their roles were reversed and the bad memories of their courtship and marriage were erased. He was almost charming, affectionate even.

"Do I dare trust him?" Toni asked herself.

Chapter 22

"Excuse me, Dr. Rossi." Bruce's client, Mr. Holton, stood in the doorway to her office, ball cap in hand. He looked upset.

"What can I do for you, Mr. Holton?" Toni got up from her desk and walked toward him.

"I'm sorry to bother you, but do you know where Dr. Bruce is? I've left him four messages on his machine, but he hasn't returned any of them. I really need to talk to him." He twisted his cap in both hands as he spoke.

"As far as I know, he is due back from his meetings in Toronto today. Let's go out and talk to Roxie, shall we?" She led Mr. Holton into the hallway toward Roxie's desk. "Any idea when Dr. Patterson is coming in, Roxie? Mr. Holton is anxious to talk to him."

Roxie patted the chair beside her desk. "Sit down, Mr. Holton. I'm just waiting for a call from him now. We'll both talk to him, okay?" Mr. Holton sat down and looked expectantly at Roxie.

Toni mouthed the words "thank you" at Roxie. 'Who was the social worker here?' she wondered. She'd have to talk to Bruce about giving Roxie a well-deserved raise. If she ever got a chance to talk to him again. Where was he, anyway?

When her last client of the morning left, she gathered her coat and bag and told Roxie she'd be back after lunch. "Thanks for putting Mr. Holton at ease, Roxie. You have a natural way with clients."

Roxie looked flustered. "Gee, Toni, I can't help it. Especially nice Mr. Holton. He was so happy when he got to talk to Bruce. I was glad to be able to do something for him."

"Did Bruce give you any idea when he would be in?" Toni crossed her fingers.

"He thought this afternoon but wasn't positive. Said he'd try his best."

"Good. Please let me know as soon as he comes in, all right?"

"No problem. Have a good lunch." Roxie turned back to her computer.

Toni walked the short distance to the restaurant that she and Max had agreed to meet at for lunch. Against The Grain was a bakery and restaurant that specialized in healthy meals and breads.

As she entered the restaurant, a great bear of a man in a police uniform rose from his seat at a table for two. She smiled and they shook hands. He took her coat and pulled out the other chair for her. After hanging up her coat, he returned to the table and thanked her for meeting with him.

"I really am grateful that you've agreed to talk with me. As you may know, Viv and I have been seeing each other for a while, and I am quite fond of her." He blushed as he said the last words.

Toni, charmed in spite of herself, leaned forward and patted his huge hand that lay on the table. "I too am very fond of her. She has mentioned you several times. You said that you are worried about her."

"Yes, very. Viv may have told you that I'm a constable with the Guelph City Police. My work often puts me in contact with people who are using drugs. When I talked to her last, she sounded disoriented. Her words were slurred, and she kept asking me to repeat myself. I asked her if she had taken any pills or smoked something. She got mad at me and hung up the phone."

Toni, concerned, asked, "You said she phoned you. Did she say why she phoned?"

"I'm not sure. She said she was in Toronto but didn't say why. Before she hung up, she said she'd probably be home in Guelph today. That was when I questioned her about drugs." He shrugged his shoulders, held his palms up, indicating that he was both perplexed and worried.

At least the timeline fit with what Bruce had told Roxie this morning, Toni reasoned. Maybe they will be home this afternoon. And maybe we'll both see Bruce and Viv.

"Officer Endicott." A large middle-aged woman waved at him from across the small restaurant.

Max smiled back. "Sorry about that. People know me from my work with kids in the school system."

"Is that how you met Viv?"

Max nodded. "Her school asked me to give my 'stranger awareness' presentation last spring. A young boy in Viv's class had been approached by someone who wanted help finding his lost kitten. Fortunately, the little boy had a feeling something was wrong and ran home. Viv knew about our program and asked her principal if I would talk to her kids. The rest, as they say, is history.

"However, we didn't actually date until Viv and her husband were living apart."

Toni decided to trust him. "I am worried about both Bruce and Viv. I hope to talk to Bruce at some point today. I not only work with him, but he and Viv have been good friends of mine for many years. Several strange things have been happening in the last week or so, and I want to make sure that I do all I can to help.

"I won't stand by and watch my friends unravel." She gave a brief outline of the events of the past week, including the car incident and the threatening email.

Max wrote down his cell number for her. "It's always on, Toni. If for some reason I don't answer, call the station and have them page me. What you've told me is worrisome, to say the least. However, without concrete proof that someone is trying to harm you, there's not much anyone can do except put some good preventative measures in place. When will your friend Hank be home?"

Toni had mentioned Hank's concerns about her safety. "He is trying to get home as soon as possible, but he's committed to book signings in cities out west until the end of the week. I don't like worrying him while he's so far away. I'm also hoping that nothing else happens."

When they finished their lunch, Max took both of Toni's hands in his as they said goodbye outside the restaurant. "I will let you know what happens with Viv when I see her, and I hope you do the same when you talk to Bruce. Please call me immediately if there are any more problems."

She was still thinking about her conversation with Max while she made dinner that evening. Viv was lucky to have him. Maybe life with Max would allow Viv to get off the rollercoaster she rode with Bruce and his problems.

As she stirred her marinara sauce, someone knocked at her back door. Toni turned to see her father standing on the back porch.

"Papa," she exclaimed with pleasure, opening the door. She hugged him and ushered him into her kitchen. Her parents rarely visited, not wanting to disturb her privacy. When they did visit, it was by invitation. She was really pleased to see her dad until she saw the expression on his face. "What's wrong, Daddy? Are you and Mama okay?"

"Somethin' happened today, *cara*. You mama don' know I'm here. But I need to tell you what happened. So I come on my own."

Toni, alarmed, sat her dad down in her rocking chair. "Tell me, Papa."

Every Monday, he and Toni's mom babysat their granddaughter, Giuliana. Her mom, Simonetta, would pick her up later on in the afternoon.

After lunch, weather permitting, Giuli and her grandmother would walk to Grange Park. Giuli would play on the swing set with the other children, and Mrs. Rossi would sit and watch on a nearby bench. This afternoon was no different. Mr. Rossi decided to work in his vegetable garden while his "girls" went off to the park.

When they reached their destination, Mrs. Rossi said she sat next to some other grandmothers she knew, intent on hearing the latest gossip while keeping an eye on Giuli. One of Mrs. Rossi's friends was having difficulty knitting a sweater for her grandson, and she bent over the stitches with her friend, untangling a complicated cable stitch. When Mrs. Rossi looked up, Giuli had disappeared.

The grandmother stood up, alarmed. "Giuli, Giuli!" she cried, hurrying around the tennis courts toward some trees at the edge of the park. She could see part of a small white running shoe behind a large maple. As she ran toward the tree, Giuli came around the tree, holding someone's hand.

"*Nonna!*" Giuli cried, a smile lighting up her face. "See who found me in the park? *Zio* James… He lost his little dog and wanted me to help find him."

Mrs. Rossi ran to the little girl, yanking her away from James and clasped her to her. "Giuli, don' ever go away without tellin' me. I din' know where you were and I was very scared." She glared at James, her look warning him to back off.

"Hi, Mrs. Rossi. Sorry to scare you. I seem to have lost the puppy I was walking for a friend." He didn't look sorry, Mrs. Rossi said later when she told her husband what had happened.

Not believing his story, Mrs. Rossi asked, "Where's the puppy's leash?" James, nonplussed at being caught in his lie, said he'd left the leash at home.

Mrs. Rossi pulled herself up to her full five feet while she issued her ultimatum. "Stay away from us, James. We don' want to see you ever again. If there is a next time, I call *Polizia*. Come, Giuliana."

Toni's father told her the story passionately, visibly upset by what had occurred. "We don' like this, Toni. We don' trust him. You mama very mad because what might've happened." His voice shook and his face had turned red.

Toni, very concerned at what her dad had told her, tried to calm him down. "I saw him this weekend, Dad, and he seemed different from when I knew him before. He told me he'd run into you at Tim Horton's and seemed happy that you'd talked to him. I'm sure he meant no harm to Giuli." As she said the words, she realized she wasn't sure at all. However, she wasn't going to let her dad hear her doubts.

"I don't want to tell you what to do, *bambina*. But I can't have you mama worried like this. If you see him again, please tell him to leave us alone. I mean it." He stood up, kissed his daughter on the cheek and left her house.

Chapter 23

Toni held the door to her office open while her last clients of the day, the Wentworths, said goodbye and headed for the double doors at the entrance to the office building. As Toni turned to go back into her office, she could hear two voices in the vestibule, one pleading, one cajoling. She paused to listen and realized that the pleading voice was Bruce's and the cajoling one was Roxie's.

"Aw, c'mon, Rox – I've always thought you were cute – what harm would it do to have a beer with an old man?" Toni inwardly cringed at the almost whining tone of her partner's voice.

Roxie's reply was very practical without being dismissive. "You're not old, Bruce, not by a long shot. You are a very attractive man with a lot to offer to the right person. That person is not me. I have always made it a rule not to mix business with pleasure. However, I am flattered and appreciate the invitation."

Toni could hear Roxie making getting-ready-to-leave noises. Would that I were that self-assured and principled as she when I was her age, Toni thought. Some very lucky guy out there was going to get a top-notch partner.

"But, honey," Bruce pleaded, "I'm all alone now. Both Viv and Sheila have made it really clear that they don't want me around any more. What am I going to do?" His voice had gone from pleading to despair.

Toni heard the steel in Roxie's reply, a nuance too subtle for Bruce, who'd obviously thrown caution out the front door. "I'm not your honey, Bruce, and I would appreciate it if you would move out of the way so that I can go home now."

Concerned lest Bruce engage in any more impropriety, Toni stuck her head around the doorjamb and asked, "Everything okay out here?" As she did so, she saw Bruce quickly withdraw his hand from the vicinity of Roxie's waist.

"Fine, fine." Bruce had the grace to look like the kid caught with his hand in the cookie jar. He moved aside so that Roxie could leave her desk.

As she passed Toni, Roxie silently mouthed 'thank you'. She smiled at Toni and said goodnight. When the front door closed behind Roxie, Toni asked Bruce to come into her office so that they could chat for a minute. She decided to say nothing about the scene she had just overheard and witnessed.

"So, Bruce, how are things going for you these days?" She was not sure what kind of mood he was in so left the question as open as possible.

"Not too great, if the truth be known," he replied. "My wife and my girlfriend both seem to have dumped me, and I really can't figure out why. I'm such a nice guy – why are they being so mean to me?" He sounded truly puzzled, as if his bizarre behaviors of late couldn't have consequences that would cause the disappearance of the two women who tolerated him. He really didn't understand, Toni thought. Unbelievable.

"Bruce, I have a friend at the U who would be a good sounding board for you and what's been happening lately." Toni knew enough not to employ the "t" word. An unfortunate number of therapists saw themselves as impervious to the types of problems their clients presented. As experts in therapy with others, they couldn't imagine that they might also need help, occasionally. If, God forbid, they had some "small" problem, they knew they could work it out on their own. Often without much success.

As predicted, Bruce bristled. "A therapist? Why would I want to do that? I saw one a while back, and it certainly didn't do me any good – in fact, I knew more than she did."

Toni changed the subject, knowing that now was not the time to bring up the strange behaviors that she and Viv had observed, to say nothing of the most recent scene with Roxie. "How about a leave of absence? I could cover some of your clients, and it might be a good time to terminate some who've become too dependent on 'Dr. Bruce', as you have often told me." As a therapist, Bruce had an unprofessional habit of creating too much dependency in some of his clients. Similar, Toni thought, to his own dependency needs. He made himself available twenty-four hours a day and even gave out his personal cell number to some of his more needy clients.

"I'll think about it, Toni. I've got some things to attend to. Maybe I'll take the next few days off and come back in on Monday. Would you talk to Viv for me? I can't seem to reach her and I need to talk to her as soon as possible."

Toni said she would, and Bruce left her office, looking relieved at going away from her presence and the questions he didn't want to answer, the problems he wanted to not only avoid but even to acknowledge.

As she walked home, she puzzled over Bruce's behavior. Bruce might very well be on the verge of a breakdown. I can't force him to talk to anyone, more's the pity. Toni felt helpless in the face of her friend's obvious need.

Rounding the corner of Glasgow Street, she could see someone sitting on her front veranda, arms wrapped around their knees, rocking back and forth in what looked like an attempt at self-comfort. She realized it was Viv. Toni said hello and asked if she'd been waiting long while giving her friend a hug.

"Not long, Toni. I knew you'd be home soon." Viv didn't look good. Her face was drawn and pale, she'd lost weight, and her usually impeccable hair was flat to her head and greasy-looking. "Can I come in for a short while? I promise not to be too long – you've probably got all kinds of stuff to do this evening." She looked desperate.

"Of course, sweetie. I'm not busy tonight… Let me feed Humphrey and put a kettle on for tea." She unlocked the door and they entered the kitchen. Toni fed her starving kitty and as she filled the kettle with water, the phone rang. Viv took over the tea preparations while Toni answered the phone.

"Hi, sweetheart." Hank's welcome voice filled Toni's head, knocking out the troubles of her day. "How are you doing? I hope things are settling down." This last was said with emphasis.

Toni felt the huge smile that lit up her face. "Hi there, yourself. Things seem to be okay right now. Viv and I are making tea and Humphrey is eating his kibble at an alarming rate. How are things up there?" She was dying to ask about Athabasca and James but didn't want to involve Viv in what had been happening lately with her ex-husband.

"Interesting, lovey. I've only been able to talk to the administration so far, but it seems that our boy is on indefinite medical leave, cause unknown, naturally, due to 'privacy concerns'." Toni could picture his quotation marks that accompanied this last phrase. "Tomorrow, I have an appointment with the head of the English department, so we will see if he is any more forthcoming with information. But I won't keep you. Say hello to Viv, and when you go to bed tonight, wrap your arms around your pillow and know that I am with you in more ways than one."

When she hung up the phone, she was still grinning and could feel the flush on her face. Viv noticed, saying, "You love him, don't you, Toni? He seems like such a good man. Don't make him wait too long, sweetie." She handed Toni her mug of tea.

The two friends sat in the kitchen, drinking tea and sharing confidences. It was almost like earlier days, except that as Viv talked about Bruce's behavior in Toronto, Toni became more disturbed than she had been earlier in the day. Viv said that his manic moods were coming more quickly and that they were more explosive than before. And she was sure that he had put something in her drink one night to make her feel groggy. Her memories of the evening were fuzzy, but she did remember Bruce threatening to throw himself off the balcony of their hotel in Toronto. She couldn't remember why he'd said it; she was only relieved that he didn't carry out his threat. She knew they had sex but couldn't remember any details.

However, when she finally awoke in the morning, there was a fair amount of blood on the sheets.

Toni, by now really alarmed, said, "Viv – you need to stop seeing him. I want you to promise me that you'll phone your lawyer first thing tomorrow morning and tell him that you want a restraining order against Bruce. I mean it. This has gone too far, and your health and well-being are compromised by continuing to see him."

'No more "Ms. Nice Guy" therapist,' Toni thought. The situation between Viv and Bruce was reaching crisis proportions, and something had to be done to stop this immediately. She'd be damned if she would stand by and do nothing.

Viv saw the determination and worry on her friend's face and promised to do what Toni said.

When Viv left, Toni called James. "I heard what happened in Grange Park yesterday, James. Tell me your side of it, please." She didn't mean to go on the attack, but she was still upset at what her father had told her and hated seeing James involve her parents and niece in his games.

"I'm not sure what was disturbing about yesterday in the park, dear. I was walking a small dog that belongs to one of my neighbors. All of a sudden, Giuli saw me and ran toward me. We were talking about the dog, which had just trotted behind a large tree, when your mom came running toward us, screaming Giuli's name. There was no cause for such a commotion." His voice was indignant, as if he were the offended party.

Toni remembered how much James had hated cats and dogs when they were married, pretending all kinds of allergies that he somehow didn't seem to develop at other people's homes in the presence of felines and canines. She had wanted a small companion so much. "What kind was it?"

"What kind was what?" James asked.

"The dog, James."

"I have no idea. Some mutt, I guess." She didn't believe him.

She also realized that he'd mentioned a neighbor in relation to the dog. He had told her he was staying at the hotel near the U, where she had dropped him off after their dinner together. What was he doing at the other end of town, walking a neighbor's dog?

She didn't trust herself to say anything else and hung up.

Chapter 24

A loud noise made Toni sit up in bed, clutching the blanket to her chest. She realized that it was her phone buzzing and grabbed it before it buzzed again. "Hello?" She peered at the time on the phone – 3.27 a.m. She said hello, again. Suddenly, Fred's voice came on the line.

"Toni?" He sounded distraught.

"Fred? What's wrong?"

"I'm in jail – I didn't know who else to call. They say that I can go home in the morning, but I will have to post bail… Could you…" His voice trailed off.

"Yes, I will come. What time can I get you?" She tried to keep the distress out of her voice, knowing that she needed to be as calm as possible in order to help her brother.

"They say eight this morning. I'm at the main station in Guelph, on Wyndham Street. I can't talk much longer."

"I will be there at eight, sweetie. Try not to worry. I'll be there." As if he would not worry, she thought. What on earth happened? This incarceration has to have something to do with Laura, she realized. Her brother had never had any trouble with the law or police. In fact, before he began working with his dad in the construction business, he had thought about joining the auxiliary police force for a time. Something terrible must have happened.

Unable to go back to sleep, Toni brewed some coffee and sat in her kitchen rocker, waiting for dawn to rise, waiting impatiently for the time to pass so that she could rescue her beloved brother from jail. She was having trouble imagining what had happened, what chain of events could have allowed this to come about, how Fred must be feeling. She stroked Humphrey and rocked, wondering, worrying.

The wall clock finally crept along to seven a.m. Toni took a quick shower and dressed. She felt tired, but her indignation and worry about Fred kept her moving forward. She grabbed her purse and headed for the police station, arriving in the parking lot at 7.53. She was standing outside the main entrance when an officer unlocked it at eight a.m., and she told the desk officer why she was there. A few minutes later, after filling out forms and writing a large check for her brother's bail, Fred appeared at an inner door and was escorted into the area where Toni was waiting for him. She went silently into his arms, looked up into his haggard face and said, "Let's get out of here."

Seated in the kitchen of Fred's house, coffees in hand, Toni asked Fred what happened.

He ran his hand over his face and cleared his throat. He looked haunted.

"I was at home on Sunday, missing my kids, not knowing how I was going to survive the inevitable court and lawyer stuff, the delays, the frustration. I just wanted it to be over, for things to be resolved, to hold my kids in my arms again. I was feeling awfully sorry for myself.

"I decided to take a drive out to Arkell, just to drive down the street where they all were, at Laura's parents' house. On the off-chance I might catch a glimpse of them, my babies. I knew I wasn't thinking rationally, that I might be causing myself trouble, but I didn't care, Toni. I just had to see them. The urge was so strong it propelled me out the door, into my car. I drove to their street and slowed down when I came near the house, where my kids were so close and yet so far away from me now. As I passed by the front of the house, I saw Laura come out of the front door, carrying Peony in her arms and holding Georgie's hand. I was so shocked at actually seeing my kids I slammed on the brakes and just sat there, staring. All of a sudden, Laura began screaming and I could see her clutching her phone and taking a picture of me and my car. I realized what was happening, stepped on the gas and turned the corner onto the next street. I pulled over, stopped and sat in the car, sobbing. A few minutes later, I became more rational and drove home.

"Laura must have called the police to report what happened, that I had violated the restraining order, that she was terrified that I meant to harm her and the kids, etcetera. Lord knows what she said. I sat at home, waiting, knowing that what I'd done was stupid, that I would most likely be charged. And not caring, frankly, what happened. I think I must've reached the lowest point I could have in my feelings that evening, sitting in my house, waiting for whatever was going to happen. I must have passed out on the couch in the living room, because suddenly I heard a loud banging on the front door. I stumbled to the door and opened it to two large uniformed City of Guelph policemen.

"Mr. Frederick Rossi?"

"Yes?" I replied.

"We have a warrant for your arrest."

"One of the officers held out a pair of handcuffs while the other one instructed me to turn around. They led me to their cruiser and helped me into the back seat. After a lot of delays and paperwork at the station, I was allowed my phone call and led to a holding cell until this morning. I know what I did was irresponsible."

Toni held up her hand to stop him. "Freddo, don't even start. The whole situation is so terrible that it hardly bears talking about. Anyone in your position would have done the same thing or at least have wanted to. Aching with every bone in your body to be reunited with your children is the most normal, understandable feeling in the world. No one would ever condemn you for those feelings. No one.

"What we need to do now is called damage control. And the best person for that lovely job is Larry, your lawyer." She pulled her phone out of her purse.

Chapter 25

Hank's appointment with Dr. Ethan Blackwood, professor of English Literature and head of the same department at Athabasca University, wasn't until eleven a.m., a good fifteen minutes from now. Hank walked slowly through the campus, admiring the original buildings, most of which were age-darkened red brick with multi-paned windows and gabled fronts. Large wooden doors with old hinges and doorknobs completed the impressions of both age and authority.

Further along the cobblestone walkway, a line of rather brutalist 1960s bunker-type buildings appeared. These contrasted sharply with the charm of the original ones. Hank hoped that his meeting with Dr. Blackwood would not be in one of the newer buildings. He turned away from these "affronts to his sensibility" and admired the ancient trees that lined the playing fields. Unlike the maples and oaks at home, most of these trees had lost their brilliant leaves in preparation for a long northern winter. Scraps of leaves skittered about the walkway as he headed for his meeting. The smell of winter was in the air. Hank pulled up his fur-lined collar, wishing he had brought a toque.

As he approached the building, he breathed a sigh of relief; no concrete bunkers for the English department. This building was a delight – more cottage-like than the others. The remains of ivies clung to the bricks and threatened to enter the building along with Hank. A pleasant-looking middle-aged woman in a twin-set was tapping a computer so quickly Hank could barely see her individual fingers. She looked up at Hank, giving him a glimpse of enormous liquid-brown eyes above the rims of her reading glasses. She smiled. "Yes?"

Hank, nonplussed by her eyes, introduced himself and asked for Dr. Blackwood. Her name plate read "Mrs. Dolores Tillinghurst". She rose abruptly from her desk, walked over to a closed door that read "Dr. Ethan Blackwood", rapped on the door and called out to her boss, "Your eleven o'clock is here, Dr. B."

The response, "Thanks, Mrs. T.," was, surprisingly, given in a southern-American drawl. The door opened, and a very tall, very slender white-haired man entered the secretary's room. He held out his hand to Hank's, which he shook with enthusiasm while taking an aromatic-smelling pipe out of his mouth with his other hand. "Welcome, welcome, Dr. Epstein. Y'all come on in… I'm Ethan, by the way… Mrs. T., please bring us a tray of coffee with all the fixin's."

Hank, disarmed by the accent and the lack of formality, relaxed. He hadn't known what to expect, but Dr. Blackwood was a pleasant surprise. "Please call me Hank, Ethan. And thank you so much for seeing me at such short notice."

Dr. Blackwood waved his hand dismissively and gestured for Hank to sit at a low coffee table flanked by two handsome leather chairs, each of which showed much age and offered a degree of comfort lacking in current models of supposedly-leather chairs. Ethan took a moment to relight his pipe while peering over his reading glasses at Hank, his wise-looking eyes holding both assessment and curiosity. "What, pray tell, brings you to this back-of-beyond neck of the woods? Your reputation precedes you with much acclaim, and I am wondering, to what do I owe this honor?"

Hank, wondering himself how he should proceed to answer,

immediately decided that honesty was the best policy. Before he could begin, Mrs. Tillinghurst bustled in with a tray of coffee items and a plate of shortbread cookies. "Thank you, Mrs. T. – don't know what we'd do without you," Ethan said, offering up a charming smile to his secretary, who, even though used to his ways, seemed flustered as she made a hasty retreat and left the office, closing the door quietly behind her. "Great gal – the last of a dying breed, unfortunately. Now, where were we?" As he spoke, he poured coffee for Hank and himself.

Hank said that he had deliberately added Athabasca University to his book tour itinerary in hopes of speaking with Dr. Blackwood about a faculty member who had appeared in Guelph, apparently on leave of absence. Hank mentioned James' name and gave Ethan a brief description as well. "He is the ex-husband of a good friend of mine, who is quite concerned about both James' behavior and the state of his health. I told her that I would make some inquiries on her behalf, as she is worried about him. James' full name is James Barrington the Third."

Dr. B. leaned back in his chair, one leg crossed over the other, puffing thoughtfully on his pipe. Smoke wreathed his head. He pulled the pipe from his mouth, looked at it for a moment and then laid the pipe in the ashtray beside his chair. "Well, well," he said, again looking thoughtful, as if he were unsure how to answer Hank. "I've been wondering how James is faring, back in the bosom of civilization, as it were. He had been having some health issues for a while and had also been mourning the loss of a great friend of his. His work had not really been suffering but was clearly missing in the enthusiasm and attention to detail that had previously been a hallmark of his value as a teacher and colleague here. When he suggested a leave of absence this past summer, I thought it a good idea at the time. What sort of things is your friend concerned about with respect to James, may I ask?"

Hank answered the question as briefly as he could, liking the professor but not wanting to divulge specific details about James' odd behaviors. "He has been in touch with my friend, his ex-wife, a few times, and she has noticed some behaviors not consonant with his former ones. He entered her house without permission and seemed to be part of a demonstration at the University of Guelph. He is also taking a keen interest in my friend's family, something he'd never previously done. Her parents are concerned, as well. I would like to reassure her, if possible, that his motives are not something to be worried about. There is also the matter of his health, which appears to be deteriorating each time he appears. Much coughing, poor appetite, etcetera." Hank waited for a response from Ethan.

Ethan leaned forward and fixed Hank with an appraising eye. "I'm unable, as I'm sure you understand, to give you any information about the state of James' health. Privacy concerns, etcetera, don't you know – ridiculous as they may be. James was receiving some treatment while he was here… As to his behavior, I'm at a loss. He seemed almost aloof while he was here on faculty. His work was impeccable – he regularly published articles in his specialty, ones received by his peers with much anticipation and interest. His lectures were well attended, but his interaction with his students was minimal and rather frosty, if anecdotal reports can be trusted. I realize that there was some trouble at his previous workplace, but because of his stellar scholarly reputation, we decided to offer him a position in spite of the troubles. I don't regret the decision and was sorry to see him leave, even if only for a short while. I'm afraid that I can't offer more information than that. And I'm sorry that you've come all this way for nothing."

Hank was sorry, too but tried to hide that fact as he offered his hand to Dr. Blackwood while they headed toward the door. He turned as he was leaving and thanked Dr. Blackwood for seeing him and asked that if anything else came to mind that might be of interest to please give him a call. The professor said he would and they shook hands again.

Chapter 26

Larry, Fred's lawyer, proceeded to read Fred the riot act, as it were, for contravening the explicit instructions of the restraining order, all the while sympathizing with his distraught client and his yearning to be reunited with his young children. He again outlined the instructions of the order and made sure that Fred understood the consequences of further contravention. Fred, now feeling like a fool, promised that he would obey. Larry again underscored the seriousness of what Fred had done and the worsening consequences for his client should he behave so foolishly again. He also instructed Fred to develop a modicum of patience while he, the lawyer, did what was necessary to make sure that Fred's case would be heard in court as soon as was humanly possible, all the while knowing that backlogs and more important matters would always impede any timeline.

To Fred, of course, the waiting was almost unbearable. He promised Toni that he would do everything possible to be as patient as he could be. He immersed himself in his work, talked to Toni and his parents often and began a diary of his feelings and thoughts, something he'd never done before. At the end of the day, when he had run out of activities that would keep his mind from brooding about his children, he would return home to his empty house in the east end of Guelph, make himself some tea and begin jotting down his thoughts, fears and hopes for the future. When he began the writing, he had no goal in mind, no plan about what he would do with his notes. He only knew that the act of writing seemed to help him in some small, barely understood way. The writing soothed some of the desperation that haunted him much of the time.

When, before bedtime, he reread what he'd written each evening, he often discovered feelings that he had not been aware of prior to his writing. The act of writing seemed to take on a life of its own and lead him down paths he'd never before traveled.

He told Toni, "Some of what I write is about my relationship with Laura and how, in retrospect, the ending was there, right in front of me, at the very beginning. I, of course, beguiled and in love, had paid no attention. I am determined now that things will be very different, going forward in my life."

Toni, hearing what Fred was doing, was again amazed at how introspective and insightful her big brother could be. He had always armored himself with physical activities and what Toni thought of as typical young guy stuff – an inordinate interest in cars, rock-and-roll and girls. And lots of beer. He had seemed to settle down after he'd met Laura and begun his apprenticeship with their dad, the goal being that Fred would take over the construction business so that their dad could enjoy his retirement before it was too late. Fred had come on board with great enthusiasm and lots of new ideas, armed with his degree in civil engineering from the U. He had brought some of his fellow engineers in for consultations and contracting and was determined to put Rossi Construction on the map as one of Southern Ontario's best construction companies. His plans and dreams were well underway when Laura left with their children.

Now, as he put down his evening's writing and drank the last of his tea, he felt himself questioning the course of his life and its priorities. He knew that life had pulled the rug out from underneath him, but he had no idea where he would land. One of the worst feelings about where he was at present was the utter lack of control over what was happening.

"Toni, if only I'd had some say in what Laura did, but I didn't, and I know that as bleak as the situation is at present, I will have to react and plan for the future as best I can. I'm counting on Larry, my lawyer, to help as much as possible and to bring Georgie and Peony back to me however he can. I am counting on him, sis. He's all I have."

Chapter 27

The lights of Guelph Place, a large banquet hall off Woodlawn at the north end of Guelph, illuminated the parking lot as Toni drove her car into one of the few remaining parking spots. She turned to her passengers, Viv and Max. "Looks like a full house tonight. Let's hope the center benefits from it."

The evening, an annual event for the university's Sexual Education Centre, fell on Hallowe'en this year, and the large convention center was decorated appropriately, if a little extravagantly, Toni thought. As she handed her coat to a hat-check person dressed as a skeleton, she couldn't help a shiver that ran through her at the memory of the night she was nearly run down by the car on Glasgow Street. She entered the large banquet hall and headed straight for the bar, determined to put that memory out of her mind.

"*Ciao, bella!*" someone behind her called as she waited in line for a glass of wine. Puzzled, she turned and saw behind her the bearded face of Devon Matheson, beaming at her in his kindly, professorial manner, his eyes full of both wisdom and merriment.

"Devon – how good to see you here. I've been meaning to call you, actually. How are you doing? And what's new in the department?" Devon was a professor in the Couples and Family Therapy Centre at the university. He had been Toni's thesis advisor and her friend for many years.

"Let's get some wine and I'll fill you in." She and Devon

managed to find a quiet corner and they talked about their respective work for a few minutes.

Although they might go for months without talking, when they did come together, by phone or in person, they were instantly in step with each other, as though they had spoken moments before. She always felt at ease with Devon. No matter what they were discussing, Toni never felt judged or criticized and knew that she could speak honestly about the topic at hand. These same qualities were what made Devon one of the most sought-after therapists in Guelph.

"Why were you going to call, Toni?" His eyes were full of both curiosity and concern.

Toni relaxed under his gaze and gave him an abbreviated version of what had been happening lately with Bruce. She described his erratic behavior both at work and toward her and Viv, his violent behaviors and emotional flip-flops, his attempted seduction of Roxie, and his trip to Toronto with Viv. "Viv has finally taken some steps toward independence from Bruce. She had the locks changed on her house, got an unlisted phone number and instructed her lawyer to get a restraining order against Bruce. I think she now realizes that her well-being could be in jeopardy if she continues to have contact with him.

"The reason why I was going to call you, Devon, was to seek some advice about how best to deal with Bruce. We are still in a loose partnership, and I guess I'm feeling a bit out of my depth. Bruce and I have been friends for so long. It's difficult to separate my personal feelings for the man from my professional concern, and it would be helpful to hear your opinion. I know you've met Bruce a few times, but you would lend an objectivity in this situation that I'm finding hard to maintain. I've also recommended to Bruce that he see you as a client."

Devon was silent for a few minutes after Toni finished. He waited to be sure that Toni had no more to add. "I'd be happy to see him, Toni. It sounds as though you've gone as far with the whole situation as you can. Your advice to Viv, moreover, is bang on. She needs to stop enabling Bruce and to not only protect herself from him but to also move toward some much-needed independence… Or, as a friend so charmingly put it, 'Get a life, already.'

"In my experience with Bruce's type of personality disorder, however, I must warn you that treatment is not only difficult but downright impossible in a lot of cases. Because they tend to see their problems as external to themselves rather than internal, therapy can be a waste of time. If none of your problems is your fault (they are always someone else's fault), why are you the person who needs to change? Additionally, because borderlines are so dependent upon other people and yet are so mistrustful of those they depend on, this ambivalent attitude usually undermines any real therapeutic relationship. All that said, though, I am certainly willing to talk to Bruce."

"Well, Devon, maybe what I'm asking is unrealistic now that I've talked to you. I did suggest that he talk to a friend of mine at the U, and he reacted in the way you just described. He was indignant when I made the suggestion, saying that he's tried therapy once, it hadn't done him any good, and that he, Bruce, knew more than the therapist anyway. End of discussion. You can lead the horse to water, however…"

The evening's festivities were about to begin, and Toni and Devon moved toward their respective seats. In parting, Devon told Toni to give him a call whenever she needed to or just to say hello. She promised that she would, thanked him and took her place at the head table.

The evening flew by with good food, blessedly few speeches, lots of talk, laughter and surprises. Part of the evening was taken up with a silent auction. Toni always donated an hour of therapy to the auction. This year, the hour was won by one of the student volunteers at the center. The final announcement of the evening was the door prize, donated by West Jet. The airline donated two round-trip tickets to any of its current locations. When the winning number was announced, Toni heard an excited cry from a table in front of her. A beaming Viv stood up, bent to give Max a kiss and went up to the podium to claim the prize.

She turned and waved the winning tickets at Toni, who applauded enthusiastically with the rest of the audience. Good for you, sweetie, Toni thought. Clapping for her friend, she thought that it was about time something wonderful happened in her friend's life. Maybe it was an indication of better times ahead. She fervently hoped so.

Viv and Max talked non-stop all the way to Viv's house, on the other side of Guelph, about where they might go and when. Viv was promulgating the excitement of Montreal, Max the bucolic serenity of the Maritimes. Toni hadn't seen Viv this happy in a long time. "Goodnight, you two – and congratulations again. This couldn't have happened to anyone more deserving than you, Viv." She hugged her friend hard.

"Thanks, Toni. It's a wonderful prize, in more ways than one. I'll talk to you soon." She and Max walked to her house, unlocked the door, waved at Toni and disappeared into the house.

When Toni arrived home, there was a large package on her back stoop, addressed to her. There was no return address on the package. Puzzled, she bent down and lifted the package up. There was a gurgling noise inside. She balanced the package on her hip while unlocking the door. Once inside her house, she put the package on the kitchen table, played with Humphrey for a bit, made herself a cup of tea and turned back to look at the package. Taking a knife from the drawer, she slit open the brown wrapping paper and then drew down the duct tape that held the edges of the box together. Whatever was gurgling was wrapped in lots of shredded bits of paper, which she reached through. She managed to lift a heavy glass jar out of the papers and held it up so that she could see what was inside.

In the half-filled jar, there floated a tiny human fetus.

Chapter 28

She set the cup down on her desk, tea sloshing into the saucer. She saw that her hand was trembling as she opened the piece of paper that was under the bottle. A photograph dropped in her lap. It was a picture of a young child, sitting on Santa's knee. Toni stared at the photo, her mind blank.

There was something vaguely familiar about the child's face, but the memory eluded her. "Think, Antonia," she chided herself. A child's bonnet was tied under its chin, hiding whatever hair it had.

The child was wearing old-fashioned clothing: a white dotted Swiss blouse under a dark-green velvet jumper. The tiny sleeves were gathered and puffed at the shoulder. The child's hand was clasped in Santa's big one.

Who is this? What is it supposed to mean? She turned the photo over. Two words, in capital letters, were printed in dark ink: MERRY CHRISTMAS.

Distracted, she glanced at her cell phone and noticed a text message. It read, "Like my present, Toni? Till we meet again…" The sender was *loosecannon…*

What? Toni was shaking her head when she realized her home phone was ringing. She lifted the receiver, not daring to say anything.

"Hello? Hello? Toni, are you there?" Hank's voice, worried, sounded in her ear, a very welcome break from the tension that had invaded her body in the last few minutes.

"Hank, thank God, yes, I'm here." She tried to keep the relief out of her voice, to no avail.

"Lovey, what's the matter? You sounded very frightened. Has something happened today? Please, talk to me." He spoke quickly, urging her to share her fear with him.

"It's probably nothing, Hank." She told him about the bottle and the message.

While she was recounting the events of the past few minutes, she realized what had been bothering her about the child. "I just figured out what's weird about the photograph. The child's face is masculine-looking, but the clothing is that of a little girl. Both the face and the clothing look familiar."

"This is not good, sweetie, whatever it is. Whoever is sending this stuff is trying to tell you something in a very peculiar fashion. I don't like it at all. Can you stay somewhere else tonight? Your parents', Viv's?"

Toni explained briefly about not being in her parents' good graces at the moment and about leaving Viv and Max at Viv's house a little while ago.

"I'm okay, Hank, really. I've set the alarm system and Humphrey and I will keep guard against all comers, benign or otherwise." She tried for a level of confidence she wasn't feeling.

"Antonia." His voice was firm, uncompromising. "Take Humphrey, turn out all the lights in your apartment and the two of you go upstairs to mine. Turn on all the lights so that if anyone is contemplating anything, they will think I'm home and you're not. I often write at night, and it's not unusual for my lights to be on into the wee hours. My car is in the driveway, so it appears that I am home. Promise me."

Toni didn't dare say no when she heard the steel in his voice. She knew that any protestation would be useless. "Okay, Hank.

It does sound like a better idea than staying downstairs alone tonight. But I can't stay in your apartment alone for long."

"You won't have to, honey. I'm coming home in a day or so." Toni felt relief flood through her...

After they said a very prolonged and loving goodnight, Toni sat at her desk, staring at the image, trying to remember why it looked so familiar. All of a sudden, she put her hand over her mouth to stifle an exclamation of dismay.

The child's face was James', taken from one of the photos he'd grabbed the night he broke into her apartment.

The clothing was hers. Her mother had made the blouse and jumper for Toni when she was three years old.

He'd combined the face and clothing, probably in a crude attempt to show Toni what their aborted child would've looked like.

Toni scooped up Humphrey, turned out all the lights in her apartment and ran up the front stairs to Hank's apartment. She slammed the door closed, threw the bolts shut and sank to the floor, burying her face in Humphrey's fur.

Chapter 29

She released Humphrey from her embrace and watched him trot into Hank's kitchen in search of those smells that fascinated felines everywhere. As she stood up, she could hear her telephone ringing faintly from her apartment downstairs. It stopped after a few rings. Her mind immediately went to the gruesome contents in the packaged bottle that she had received earlier. She had put the package and its contents on the shelf in the hall closet, determined to put both out of her mind, if at all possible. She would show them to Hank when he got home.

What bothered her was the fact that someone not only wanted to send her a message in a particularly disturbing way but also knew where she lived. James' face kept haunting her. She was as certain as she could be that the signature, *loosecannon*, was her ex-husband's way of letting her know that he would be coming at her with no restraints. She would be much relieved when Hank returned from his tour.

She glanced at the mantel clock over Hank's living room fireplace. Twelve fifteen a.m. She remembered the ringing phone from a few moments earlier. Who would be calling her at that time of night? Without thinking, she turned toward the door to the stairs that went back to her apartment. No, Toni, she admonished herself. You promised Hank that short of a fire, earthquake or the Zombie Apocalypse, you would not venture down those stairs until morning.

She spent the next few minutes roaming through the

apartment, touching things, opening closets, breathing in the faint scent of Hank that lingered on some of his clothing. She giggled at one point, realizing that she was behaving like a love-sick teen, desperate for any hint of the object of her unrequited obsession. Her alter ego finally stepped forward. Stop it, you fool… Go to bed.

Toni almost tripped over Humphrey as he sauntered out of the bathroom, where he had been drinking copious amounts of water from the toilet bowl. His whiskers were dripping. She saw him disappear into the kitchen, where Hank always kept a litter box and kibble for the cat. When she and Hank were both home, Humphrey was allowed to wander freely between the two apartments.

Toni got ready for bed, changing into an old shirt of Hank's, brushing her teeth, turning out the bathroom light and setting down a bowl of fresh water in the kitchen for Humphrey. Humph might not be picky about his sources of water, but his mistress certainly was. She left the rest of the apartment's lights on, as Hank had suggested. Heading down the hallway to Hank's bedroom, she paused to study the many framed photographs that lined the walls. One in particular caught her attention. It was a photo of Hank, his arm around a beautiful woman. They were gazing at each other, smiling with happiness.

Toni staggered back a step, her hand flying to her mouth as she suppressed a gasp. It was the same woman who was on the front porch the other night, the one who had dinner with Hank at The Other Brother's. She peered at the photo more closely, realizing that the photo was worn in spots and had been creased at some point. Hank was sporting mutton-chop sideburns. He also had considerably more hair than now, and his pants were bell bottoms, last popular in the seventies and early eighties. Toni relaxed a bit as she took the framed picture off its hook and turned it over. The writing on the back read, "Hank and Aviva, honeymoon in Israel, 1984." She then noticed the desert-like background.

Dummy, she chided herself. You've just wasted how much time and energy worrying about his ex-wife? Hank had told her that he and Aviva were good friends and that they saw each other for dinner occasionally. Toni was very fond of Rachel, their fifteen-year-old daughter, who stayed with Hank whenever she came home from her Toronto boarding school and their schedules coincided. She shook her head, as if to dispel the last vestiges of jealousy. "Idiot. Would you respect him as much as you do if he still simmered with hatred over his ex-marriage the way so many of your clients do? Don't think so, Toni."

She settled into Hank's large four-poster bed, tucking flannel sheets and quilts around her. Humphrey stretched out his full length beside her and gave a very contented purr. Her eyes were closing as the phone downstairs began to ring again. This time it rang until the machine picked up. Please don't tell me this will go on all night, she fretted.

It did. The phone rang at least once an hour for the remainder of the night.

Toni's sleep was fitful and as she got out of bed at her usual time, she felt groggy with the beginnings of a headache. Great. Today will be merely something to be got through, she thought.

While working on case notes on her office computer, she heard voices in the hallway. Her office door was open, but she couldn't see the two people conversing. However, she recognized the voices immediately.

"Bruce, what happened to you?" Roxie sounded concerned.

"It's nothing, Rox. You should see the other guy." Bruce

sounded happy, almost self-satisfied.

"It can't be 'nothing'. Your arm is in a sling and your hand is all bandaged up."

"I fell and banged up my hand. Nothing to worry about. The doc says it'll be good as new soon. I've just come to pick up some files. I'll be working at home for the rest of the day."

Toni heard Bruce head up the stairs to his office. After a few minutes, she heard him descend the stairs, say goodbye to Roxie and leave the building. Toni tried to put the conversation out of her mind for the rest of the working day.

That evening, settled on Hank's couch, she called Viv. Toni listened with growing alarm as her friend told her what had really happened to Bruce.

"He was wild, Toni. I've never seen him so angry. I thought he'd accepted the fact that we were separated and I am involved with Max. He hadn't wasted any time going after Sheila, after all. I guess I was wrong. When I told him about Max and my upcoming vacation, he went berserk. He picked up a kitchen chair and threw it at the ceiling, yelling at me the whole time. His face was so red I was afraid he'd have a stroke or a heart attack. He paced up and down the length of the kitchen, saying awful things about Max, and at the end of his tirade, he slammed the side of his hand into the cupboard. His wedding ring left a dent in the wood.

"When it became clear that he'd done some damage to his hand, I took him to the General. The emergency-room doctor said the X-ray showed that a bone chip had broken off and was lodged in the middle of his hand. When we inquired about surgery, the doctor said it probably wouldn't help, given where the chip was located. He warned Bruce that he would be in pain for a while before the injury heals."

"How are you dealing with all of this, Viv?"

Viv's response was almost as worrisome as Bruce's behavior. "I feel so guilty, Toni. If I hadn't told him about the vacation, none of this would've happened. Max and I will just have to go some other time, I guess. Bruce is in great pain. I've given him some Tylenol 3s. I'm hoping he can sleep through the night."

Toni had called Viv's cell phone number. "Where are you, Viv?" She knew the answer before it came.

"I brought Bruce back to his apartment. He really needs someone to look after him for a while."

I bet he does, thought Toni. He's got you right where he wants you. You've canceled the holiday with Max and now you're playing nurse to poor, injured Bruce. Exactly the outcome Bruce wanted. No wonder he had sounded so happy and confident earlier today when she had overheard his conversation with Roxie.

Viv was beginning to sound defensive, as though she knew her behavior might not meet with Toni's approval. Toni signed off, telling her friend to be careful.

About all I can do at the moment, Toni thought.

As soon as she finished speaking with Viv, the phone rang. "Toni, it's Max here." He sounded worried. "I can't seem to find Viv. Have you heard from her today?"

Toni reassured him that she'd spoken to Viv and that she seemed fine. Toni would leave it to her friend to fill Max in, if that's what she chose to do. Did Max want her to leave word with Viv to call him? "Yes, please." Toni sent Viv a text asking her to call Max.

Toni crawled into Hank's bed and dropped into a deep, dreamless sleep, exhaustion taking over, finally. She was jarred awake by the sound of the doorbell ringing in sharp staccato bursts. Heart pounding, she sat up, clutching the bed clothes, and looked at the clock. One a.m. Not again, she thought. Last night it was the phone, now this. The sound stopped for a few minutes then started again.

Toni grabbed her cell phone, found Max's number and pressed "dial". A very sleepy Max mumbled, "Hello." Toni explained her problem as succinctly as she could. Once Max was satisfied that Toni was as safe as she could be in her house, he told her a patrol car would be on its way shortly and that it would drive slowly by her house at regular intervals for the rest of the night. And that she was to phone 911 if anything else happened. Toni thanked him and apologized for waking him.

Unable to sleep, in spite of her tiredness, Toni made some tea and huddled in bed with Humphrey. James had to be the person who was doing these things to her, but why? She went over the events of the past few weeks, trying to find some answers to her questions. Nothing she came up with made any sense.

She'd been trying to help Bruce; he'd been angry about the visit to his apartment but seemed to have moved on. He didn't have any reason to turn her life upside down. And James had been friendly up to the point of physical affection – she hadn't sensed any hint of dissatisfaction toward her.

Okay, Humph, she said to her sleeping kitty, time to look at these recent events logically instead of trying to brush them aside as isolated aberrations that were unconnected. She leaned over the side of Hank's bed and opened the drawer at the top of the night table. She took out the notepad that Hank always left close by in case any story ideas popped into his mind as he was drifting off to sleep. A nub of a pencil rested at the front of the drawer, and Toni sat back against the pillows and began a diagrammatic list of strange events that had happened recently. As she wrote, she became certain that much of what had been happening seemed to involve James, either directly or indirectly.

James appeared to be central to much of the disruption: his sudden and unexpected appearance in her house, for example, combined with her knowledge of his past history as a private investigator. The glimpse Toni thought she had of him in the group of anti-abortion protesters near the Sex Ed. clinic, and his limp that evening. Amber had told Toni that she had kicked the protester in the shin, the same man whom she described in terms of what could have been James' appearance to Toni. His odd behavior after their dinner together when she dropped him off at the hotel and he got into a cab instead of going to the hotel's entrance. His possible abduction of her niece, Giuli, at the park when Mrs. Rossi was taking care of her. His appearance at Tim Horton's and at Giuli's birthday party. And his denials of any negative intentions for all of these events.

When she balanced these events and others against his increasingly friendly and almost ingratiating attitude when she saw him, they didn't make sense to her. His words and treatment of her seemed to indicate that he still cared about her. So why would he be connected to the strange events that all seemed to have begun with his reappearance in her life? Think, Toni, her alter ego whispered – if James were the cause of all these negative happenings, how could he still care about you? And why does he look so awful each time you see him?

She suddenly remembered one of the old adages from her social work school days. A respected professor had dropped a truism into a conversation in class one day, one that made so much sense that Toni had a "Eureka!" moment in her mind:

"Always pay more attention to the behavior than to the words." How many times had she thought of that gem of advice in her therapy work? Pay attention to the behavioral clues as well as the words of clients. Words are easy; it's the behavior that is usually the best way of judging character. If there is consonance between the words and the behavior, chances are good someone is telling the truth. If the behavior is different than the words, watch out! She remembered how often James would tell her he loved her, only to turn around and do something that contradicted those words. Such as denigrating her in front of his colleagues; or having an affair; or disrespecting her decision to terminate her pregnancy. Good old cognitive dissonance, Antonia. Staring you in the face all these years.

She put down her pencil and paper, gathered Humphrey in her arms and let her mind wander. If he really did care about her, why would he be undermining his positive feelings with so many negative events? And what was wrong with his health? Maybe Hank would have some information when he returned from Athabasca. Her mind went around in circles for what seemed like hours.

Finally, as dawn was beginning its journey over the horizon, Toni fell into an uneasy sleep.

Chapter 30

Viv snuggled up against Max as she recounted her last meeting with Bruce. She looked up at Max, debating whether she could be completely honest about what had happened. Max, sensing her hesitation, asked, "What's wrong, Viv? Did Bruce do something to upset you again?"

"No," Viv said. "I'm just worried that when I tell you the details, you will be angry and you will want to confront Bruce. I want to be honest with you, but I don't want to provoke you, either."

"Not to worry, sweetheart. You told me that it is finally finished, and I believe you. As much as I fantasize about pulverizing him, my rational self knows that Bruce will suffer the repercussions and get the help that he needs." Max pulled Viv to him in a close embrace and kissed the top of her head. "Please continue."

Viv had postponed her final meeting with Bruce as long as she could, but when she ran out of excuses, she knew that she couldn't put off the inevitable any longer.

She decided that she would go to his apartment instead of inviting him to meet her at her house on Metcalf. Her rationale was that if she invited Bruce to her home, and there were any problems getting Bruce to leave, she would be in trouble.

Meeting at his apartment, on the other hand, would allow her to escape more easily if she had to, It made sense to her at the time. However, driving to Bruce's, she began having doubts.

What if he tried to prevent her from leaving? She'd told Max about her intentions and knew that if she ran into any problems with Bruce, Max was only a phone call away. Her fingers were crossed, just in case. Small comfort, Viv, she told herself.

Bruce had opened the door at her first knock. He beamed at her, inviting her in, taking her coat from her, asking her what kind of wine she would like. "No wine, Bruce. I can't stay long, and I am driving." She looked around at his living room, noticing that not only was it messy but dirty, too. There were rings on the coffee table, newspapers spread open on the rug, and the smell of kitty litter was almost as prevalent as the time she and Toni had been there, looking for Bruce.

"How are you doing, Bruce?" Viv struggled not to comment on the disarray and bad smells but to do what she had resolved to do by coming there. No more Ms. Nice Guy, Viv, she told herself. You need to make him understand that our relationship is over.

"I'm fine, honey, thanks for asking." He leaned toward her from his chair and tried to take her hand. Viv moved further away from his reach, finding a place on the other end of the couch. He didn't look good. His hand was still bandaged, and his hair was greasy and uncombed, his clothes rumpled. His eyes were bloodshot and he looked tired, drawn.

"Bruce, I will keep this short, as I know you must be busy, and I have a big day at school tomorrow." She tried to sound firm. Inwardly, she was anything but. As she continued speaking, however, she gained some confidence. She knew that she'd reached a turning point and that she had to move forward. Her task at hand was to let Bruce know that their road together had come to an end.

Her voice got stronger as she continued, and she felt herself relaxing a bit. "You know that I still have feelings for you, Bruce.

We have been together for a long time and gone through a lot. I also know that our relationship has changed lately.

"We both began seeing other people after we decided to separate, and I am at a turning point in my life. I am moving forward. I also realize that our being together is not good for either of us, and trying to pretend that it is good is harming us both. I don't know what your plans are, but I know that the only way I can become a better person is by ending our relationship." She took a deep breath.

Bruce stood up abruptly and began to pace. "I don't know what you are talking about, Viv – I thought we were still a team. I thought you still loved me." He raked his good hand through his hair. He turned to face her, his face suffused with blood. "Is this that Max guy you're seeing? If it is, I'll have it out with him. I'll tell him how great we are in bed. I'll..." He was sputtering, spitting words.

Viv got up from the couch but didn't move toward him. "No, my decision doesn't have anything to do with Max, Bruce. It is about our relationship and what I know is good for me. Our being together has become very strange; I seem to be an unwitting participant in things I have no control over, and I want to begin a different path for myself. You need to get some professional help for your problems, as do I. I will always care about you, and I honestly hope that you find the direction that will allow you to become that good person I know is waiting to show itself to the world."

Bruce had fallen back into his chair, his hands hanging down between his legs. "Help me, Viv, please help me." He looked up at her; his eyes were pleading with her.

"No, Bruce. The only person who can help you is you. I'm not your therapist. I need to figure out my own way forward. Talk to Toni. I'm sure she will be able to give you some ideas about what to do. Or point you toward someone who can."

She retrieved her coat and left the apartment, closing the door firmly behind her.

Chapter 31

As she drove to her parents' home, Toni smiled as she thought about her last conversation with Hank. She had told him about the events of the night before, her call to Max and her ruminations about James. Hank was concerned but relieved that she had called the police and listened to her ideas about James.

"I agree with your suppositions about James. When you itemize the events and his seemingly random appearance in them, it makes a lot of sense that he is the author of them, so to speak. The question is why, and what his intentions are with respect to you. We'll talk as soon as I get home, love. You've given me a lot to think about. Maybe I can convince you to continue using my apartment as a refuge? For safety reasons, of course." Toni heard the smile in his voice. She felt a smile light up her own face.

"It'll be wonderful to have you home, Hank. What time does your plane get in tonight?" She deliberately left the apartment-as-refuge question unanswered.

Toni was to meet him at Pearson Airport in Toronto at ten p.m., after having dinner with her parents. "Think about my suggestion, please." Hank had turned his question into a request. She said she would.

Mrs. Rossi enfolded her daughter in a warm embrace when she stepped into her parents' kitchen. "You look *bella, bambina!*"

"So do you, Mama," Toni countered with sincerity and relief. Her mother had a smudge of flour on her cheek, her long gray hair was escaping from its bun, and her face was flushed from the heat of the kitchen. Things were bubbling in pots on the stove top, and the smells were intoxicating. To Toni, no other place in the world embodied the word 'home'. She was relieved when she realized that her mother was no longer angry with her about James and his strange behavior.

Her mother asked about Fred and his meeting with the lawyer, and Toni told her as much as she knew. She knew how difficult it was for her parents not to be able to see Fred's babies – "Maybe never again, *cara*?" Toni reassured her mama as best she could, knowing that grandparents had no legal rights to access their grandchildren. A very sorry state of affairs, in Toni's opinion. Her parents doted on their grandchildren, and to be caught in the middle of this awful custody and access battle between Fred and his wife was taking its toll on her mother, for one.

"I feel my heart ripped outta my chest, Antonia," her mama said, wiping tears from her cheeks.

"You papa and I try not to talk about it too much, but it is a terrible thing to bear. We do not deserve." Her voice was filled with sobs. She turned away from her daughter and busied herself at the stove. Toni put her arms around her mama from behind her, trying to reassure both of them.

"I am also sorry about what happened with James and Giuli, Mama. I guess James wasn't thinking straight when he disappeared for those few minutes with Giuli. I told him what an upsetting experience it was for you, and he feels bad about causing you so much worry. I'm sure it won't happen again." She reassured her mother as best she could. Would that she felt as confident about James and his disturbing behaviors as she told her mother she did.

"Not to worry, Antonia. It for sure wasn't anything to do with you. Is probably just bad luck that we were all at the park at the same time, no?" Her mama put her arm around her daughter and led her to a seat at the big table. *"Vino, cara?"* She held up a bottle of Valpolicella.

After the dinner, and giving many reassurances to her parents that she would take good care of herself, Toni set out for the airport to pick up Hank. She drove through the village of Arkell, then east on the First Line and north on County Road 20 toward Guelph Line, Campbellville and the 401.

As she headed into the big S curve on County Road 20, she eased off on the gas pedal. Her rate of speed was a bit fast for her comfort on these bends. She moved her foot to the brake. Nothing happened. Oh my God, she thought. I'm not going to make the curve. Her car shot forward, Toni desperately pumping the brake pedal. She saw the gate post just before the sound of a sickening thud of car and immoveable object.

She somehow managed to extricate herself from the inflated airbag and sat, stunned, trying to process what had just happened. She saw two people hurrying down the driveway. She opened the car door and stood as they approached the car. "You okay, miss?" An older man, dressed in coveralls and a barn jacket, looked quite concerned. The woman with him hung back a bit, not speaking but looking worried as well.

"I think I'm okay, thanks very much, but I can't say the same for your post or my car. My brakes failed on the curve." The front of her car was caved in and smoke was pouring out of the hood. She found herself shaking.

"Don't worry about the post, dear. It can be replaced, and your car can be fixed, probably." The farmer peered at the front of the car, a dubious expression on his face. "It won't be drivable for a while, at any rate. Let's go up to the house and we'll call the police."

Toni grabbed her purse from the front seat and followed the couple up the driveway. A black-and-white border collie bounded out of a shed to greet them, tail wagging furiously. He put his front paws on Toni's coat and began licking her face with great fervor. "Down, Buddy, down." At his owner's command, the dog reluctantly removed his paws from Toni's coat and trotted beside her into the farmhouse. "He likes pretty women, does old Bud. I'm George, by the way, and this here's Isabel, my wife." He pointed to his wife, who asked Toni if she would like some tea. Toni introduced herself, said she'd be most grateful for the tea. She sank into one of the old painted kitchen chairs, Buddy's head in her lap. He looked up at her in adoration.

As she absently patted Bud's head and stroked his ears, she looked around the kitchen with interest. The farm kitchen was warm and cluttered with evidence of lives lived with both love and purpose. Stacks of paper covered counters and table, and the remains of dinner and just-washed dishes hugged the sink area. A large black McLaren cook stove sent out welcoming heat and a cast-iron kettle steamed gently in the corner of the stove. An old flat-to-the-wall was crammed with mismatched dishes. Many pairs of boots encrusted with dirt sat by the kitchen door on two boot trays. Over the boots hung coats and jackets, most of which seemed in need of serious repair.

She couldn't have landed in a more welcoming environment, if one had to have an accident, she thought to herself, still in a state of disbelief at this turn of events.

Toni was very grateful that this couple had taken her into their home without hesitation and told them so. George blushed, said it was nothing that anyone else wouldn't have done and handed her an old black phone so that she could phone the police.

Once all the arrangements were made, Toni called Hank's cell phone but only reached his voicemail. George drove Toni back to her home on Glasgow Street, refusing to take the money she offered him. She resolved to give the couple something to show her gratitude for what they'd done for her. She called her parents and told her dad what had happened, assuring them she was fine, just a bit shaken. Her dad relayed Hank's message to her. He had phoned upon receiving Toni's message and was much relieved to hear she was unharmed. The police had reassured her parents of Toni's uninjured state.

"We were very worried, *cara*. Your Hank was also worried. He's on his way home with Red Car, and asks for you to stay put. Antonia, why does he sound more worried than your mama and papa? Does he know things that we don't?"

Toni attempted to downplay Hank's concerns. "He's just like that, Papa. He always worries when he's away and can't help. I think he just feels frustrated, is all." She hoped her dad believed her.

"Okay, *cara*. I hope you're right." He didn't sound very convinced. She heard a car outside and said a hasty goodbye to her dad, promising to call in the morning. She hurried to the window, but the car had not stopped in front of the house. No Hank. The phone began to ring. It was eleven thirty p.m. Who could be calling at this hour?

"Toni?" It was James. He sounded startled to hear her voice.

"What is it, James?" Toni was surprised to hear from him and wondered why he was calling.

"Are you all right? I've been trying to get hold of you all evening."

Toni checked her call display. James' phone number was not

on it. "I had a bit of an accident, but I'm okay, thanks." James expressed some half-hearted concern, although he sounded neither surprised nor worried. She found his lack of empathy disconcerting, given his earlier attention to her well-being. In addition, he didn't inquire as to the type of accident. "Curiouser and curiouser," as the author said, years ago…

"I would like you to come to dinner at my house Friday night, Antonia." It sounded almost like a demand.

"What house, James? I thought you were staying at the hotel…"

"A friend lent me his house while he is on sabbatical in Italy, some comp. lit. project for the U." Toni mentally translated this exclusionary lingo into its non-English department meaning: the fellow, a full professor with tenure, was spending a year in Italy working on a comparative literature project courtesy of the University of Guelph's deep pockets for such antiquated customs. The concept of taking a fully paid year off every seven years for professors was quickly going the way of the dodo bird at most universities in Canada. The University of Guelph was a hold-out in this respect. What a sabbatical usually meant was little work and lots of play, accompanied by much R and R and *vino*, in the case of *Italia* and its many charms.

The tone of James' voice held an imperious quality that rubbed Toni the wrong way. Charm, as Toni often noted to herself, was neither sincere nor long-lasting. "I'll have to let you know, James. I'm pretty busy right now." To say nothing of annoyed, she thought.

"Please, Toni? I'll make your favorite meal. I really need to talk to you." His tone was back to humble, almost pleading.

She heard a key in the front door. She hastily gave in to James' request, saying, "Okay, James. I'll see you then. I have to

176

go."

Toni hung up the phone and ran into the front hallway, just in time to see Hank put down his carryall and hold out his arms to her.

Chapter 32

James put down his cell phone and looked at himself in the mirror over the hall table. He looked like hell, he thought. His eyes were sunk back into their sockets, and great dark bruises extended downward on either side of his nose. His cheeks, too, were sunk inward, his complexion spotted with pustules, his pallor an unhealthy shade of gray. I look like a cadaver, James thought.

He'd lost so much weight that his clothes hung on him like a mannequin's; he'd run out of notches on his belts and had to punch in new ones to accommodate his thinness. His appetite was gone, and he was stooped over like an old man. He was thirty-eight years old.

I don't care, he thought. I have one thing left to do, and once that's done, my work in this godforsaken town is done. He smiled at himself in the mirror at the thought of accomplishing what he came here to do. The smile looked like that of a corpse. A rictus of a smile. He turned away from the mirror in disgust.

James thought of his life in Guelph in comparison with his time in Athabasca.

He had truly enjoyed his early years at the University of Guelph, his status as a professor on his way to tenure, the adulation of his young students. In contrast, his current employment at Athabasca was much less enjoyable and fraught with what he considered off-the-cuff treatment by his department head, Dr. Blackwood. His classes were a chore, especially as his health deteriorated, and his student evaluations, lackluster at best.

To say nothing of the miserably cold winters punctuated by brief summers and clouds of blackflies. He shivered thinking about all of it.

His only regret was the loss of his friend, Tim. Tim, who had understood and applauded James and his disdain for most of humanity, who encouraged James' efforts to insulate himself from the dregs of the University's population. Together, he and Tim had formed a unit of superior intellect that dissected and skewered most of those whom they saw as inferior to themselves. And the sex they shared – unlike anything he'd experienced before or since. Us against the world, Tim. How he missed his lover. His dead lover, he corrected himself.

After the catastrophe of his marriage to Toni, he rather enjoyed toying with her now, drawing her in close. His ability to charm her and others was something he'd developed over a lifetime of contempt for most of the human race. He'd learned, early on, that in order to accomplish things, to get what he wanted, he would need to dissemble before those who held power over what he desired. He'd been called a benevolent misanthrope by those who thought they understood him. The truth, in fact, was much more sinister.

His anger at Toni and her abortion, her desertion of him in the face of his firing, her ability to move on with her life with no visible repercussions for the terrible things she'd done to him, continued to stoke episodes of rage in him. The only thoughts that soothed him were his determination and plans to get even, even if they were the last things he did. His pretense of affection, his overtures of getting together with her again, were a facade that he was finding more and more difficult to maintain as time went on. His only hope was that he could accomplish his reason for being here in this godforsaken place. He was determined to see it through to the end, no matter what it cost him.

He knew his time was limited not only by this dreadful disease that was busy consuming his body and mind but by the hatred he felt for Toni and others like her. His last and greatest achievement would be to bring her to his level of self-loathing and pain. He would force her to understand that killing their baby had been the ultimate act of treason. Forgiveness was not possible. Only the utmost type of revenge would assuage the fires of rage that were consuming him.

Chapter 33

Toni clung to Hank as if he were a life preserver on a sinking ship. She couldn't remember the last time she'd been so happy to see someone.

"Are you all right, lovey?" He tipped Toni's face up to his, a worried expression on his face. Unshed tears of happiness and relief made her eyes shine. She mumbled something in response, her head tucking into the folds of his heavy winter coat. She was holding onto him for dear life, willing those tears to remain at bay. After a few minutes, she managed to compose herself, held onto his lapels with both hands and smiled up at his dear face.

"I guess I didn't realize how much I missed you," she whispered. Her voice was hoarse with emotion.

"Hallelujah!" Hank threw back his head and gave a great whoop of laughter. He picked up a startled Toni and twirled her around. When he set her back down on the rug, he kissed her for what Toni thought must've been an hour. Her head felt like it was stuffed with cotton balls. The passionate love she felt for him was unlike anything she'd ever experienced.

Upstairs, they settled on Hank's couch, Humphrey curled up blissfully on Hank's lap, an opened bottle of wine on the coffee table in front of them. Hank twirled an errant lock of hair that had escaped Toni's French braid. "Tell me what happened tonight, sweetheart."

Toni recapped her evening, beginning with dinner at her parents. When she was finished telling him everything, he gathered her in his arms. "We'll get to the bottom of this together, Toni. I want you to call Roxie in the morning and tell her you will be working from home for a while. I think we will pay Bruce an unexpected visit tomorrow. And I will be keeping a close watch when you go to James' for dinner in the evening. I can't believe that these 'accidents' are unrelated, nor do I believe in the 'disgruntled client' possibility. I'll bet my next book that the 'perp', as they say, is James. Right now, he looks like a good candidate for that '*loosecannon*' designation."

"What about your new book schedule, Hank? Can you just take time off without incurring Stella's wrath?" Toni knew how demanding Stella could be once one of Hank's new books was published. She embodied charm personified while Hank was writing, but once the initial print run was done, she turned into a veritable harridan, calling him several times a day with appointments for book signings, radio interviews and just plain old gossip about the children's book publishing industry.

"Stella actually works for me, lovey, not the other way around. I pay her very well to do what she so superbly does as an agent. There's nothing scheduled until next week, nothing that can't be postponed for a while. Stella will have to be satisfied with texts and voicemails until then. Getting to the bottom of who the bastard is that is doing these terrible things to you is much more important than book signings in Orillia." His grip on her tightened. "Now, why don't you model that old shirt of mine while I get out of these city clothes and take a shower?"

Toni awoke in the middle of the night to turn over, and Hank turned with her, his arms pulling her back against his warm solidity, his breath soft in her hair.

Their lovemaking had been soft and dream-like, full of tenderness and need, unlike the desperation of other times. When it was over, she sobbed with happiness and love. Only when sleep came did they relax fully into their close embrace of each other. She smiled now as she felt Hank pressed against her. Maybe she was learning to move beyond the damage caused by her marriage to James.

In the morning, they went for breakfast at Diana, a restaurant on Wyndham Street. Toni asked Hank about his trip and if he'd learned anything useful about James' tenure at the University.

"I had a brief meeting with the head of the English department at the University in Athabasca. Nice fellow, near retirement age, named Ethan Blackwood. Sounded like something out of Faulkner's back woods' stories. He seemed genuine, intelligent and forthcoming. Unfortunately, he doesn't know much, either. He's as puzzled by James' illness and behavior as we are. He promised to make some inquiries for me and said he'd try to get back to me by the end of this week. He did say that James' health deterioration was very gradual, and that he had been able to maintain his teaching and writing commitments. He has been granted an indefinite leave of absence from the University in Athabasca with the understanding that he would continue with as much of his work as possible while in Guelph. Another thing he told me was that James had been mourning the death of a great friend of his, someone who had died before James' leave of absence."

Toni's gaze had shifted from Hank to people passing by the restaurant window. Everyone was hurrying because of the rain. Suddenly a familiar figure passed by quickly. Toni turned in her seat to catch another glimpse.

"What is it, lovey?"

She turned to Hank, a puzzled look on her face. "I think that was James, but he looked even more ill than the last time I saw him. I wasn't sure it was him until I saw the back of his head and his gait. He looks terrible." She shook her head in sadness.

Hank reached across the table for her hand. "Try to be as objective as you can, sweetheart. This may turn out to be the man who is trying to harm you. Let's be certain either way before you waste your sympathy on the wrong person, okay?"

She nodded with reluctance. "You're right, of course." She was grateful that Hank had pulled her back to reality.

"Hey, Max, over here…" Toni saw the policeman before he saw them. She had made arrangements to meet Max at the restaurant. When introductions between Hank and Max were over and Max had his coffee in front of him, they took turns bringing Max up to date with recent events. Max suggested a tap on both phone lines on Glasgow Street as well as a bodyguard for Toni. She wasn't happy with the idea of a stranger accompanying her everywhere.

"I can probably fulfill most, if not all, of that function, Max, with pleasure." Hank smiled at Toni as he said those words. "I've postponed my schedule while we clear up this mess once and for all. But if we can avail ourselves of your back-up and help when needed, that will make our job a lot less stressful. I realize it's an unorthodox way to proceed, but until we have some concrete proof about who is doing these things to Toni, we don't have much to offer the police. Lots of hunches but no 'smoking gun', as it were."

"Awful analogy, Hank!" Toni shivered.

"Sorry, love. I wasn't thinking." He looked so contrite that Toni forgot Max's presence and blew Hank a kiss across the table.

"Stop it, you two," Max said. "You're making me jealous. I still haven't heard from Viv, Toni. Do you know where she is and how she is doing?" Max looked upset.

"Let me call her again, Max. Maybe I can reach her at school this afternoon, once classes are over. I'll call you as soon as I know anything."

Hank and Toni drove up to the north end of Guelph to Golden Triangle Collision on Dawson Road. The mechanic working on Toni's car came out to meet them in the lobby of the repair business. Max asked about the brake lines.

The mechanic wasted no time telling them. "Yup, sure looks like she's been tampered with, by jeeze. Lines are cut so that the fluid leaked out real slow, like. Seen it once before. Crikey, awful 'ting to do to someone. Youse was lucky, that's all. Coulda been a lot worse." He wiped his forehead with a greasy-looking cloth.

Hank said, "Actually, it was my friend who was driving the car when the brakes failed. Would you be willing to talk to the police about what you've found?" The mechanic said he would.

As they drove toward Toni's office on Woolwich, she was uncharacteristically silent. Hank reached over, took her hand and gave it a squeeze. "Ready, love?"

Toni nodded as they pulled into the parking lot beside her office building. She hoped that she looked less disturbed than she felt.

Chapter 34

Toni hesitated before she opened the door of the Land Rover. She turned to Hank, a look of regret on her face.

"I hate having to do this, Hank. Bruce and I have known each other for so long and have gone through so much together – school, friendship, partnership, personal problems and so on. I've always known about his personality problems, but until recently they didn't seem to interfere with his work. If anything, his borderline personality seemed to enhance his ability to empathize and connect with certain clients. But lately, that separation between his problems and his professional life has been breached and is causing major problems. He's become a liability both at work and in his private life. I'm afraid that we've reached the end of our time together, both professionally and personally."

Hank leaned over and kissed her cheek. "Let's see if you're right, love."

They hurried through the cold rain and up the steps into the building, greeting Roxie as they entered the reception area. "Hey, you two, I left a message at your house. Bruce is due in any minute, and I knew you'd want to see him, Toni."

"Thanks, Rox. We'll wait in my office until he comes in."

A few minutes later, the front door flew open and they could hear Bruce calling to Roxie as he shook out his umbrella. "Hi, beautiful! Great day, eh? I'm just here to pick up some files. Won't be a second." He ran up the stairs, two at a time, in a rush for some reason. Toni and Hank followed him up to his office.

They slipped into the room unannounced, catching Bruce by surprise.

"Hey, guys, you startled me!" He did look surprised but pleased to see them. "How did you know I'd be here? I'm supposed to be on a mini-holiday."

"I had to pick up some files, too, Bruce, and we heard you come in while I was sorting through some mail. Okay if we all sit down for a moment?" She was trying to disarm Bruce as much as possible before she began what he would most likely interpret as accusations. "Hank and I are on our way up north, actually.

"How are you doing? We haven't seen each other much, and I've been wondering how things are going." She tried to keep the tone light, casual. Old friends getting caught up.

"Great, thanks for asking." His face lit up with a huge grin. "Hasn't Viv told you? We're back together again." He hugged his injured hand to his chest. He was sorting through the mail on his desk with his good hand, searching for something.

Toni and Hank both rolled their eyes, glancing at each other. Bruce was not only disintegrating but delusional, as well. Toni knew that Viv had said a final goodbye to her ex-husband. Both she and Hank were thinking, "Oh my God. I don't believe it." Toni knew that what Bruce was saying was not only wrong but wishful thinking.

"Have you contacted Devon Matheson yet?" Toni avoided what Bruce had just said and tried to keep her voice non-judgmental.

"Why are you still going on about that, Toni? I don't have any reason to see a therapist. I told you that when you suggested it. Stop seeing problems where there aren't any." His face was clouded with indignation.

Hank interrupted, "Where were you two nights ago, Bruce?"

"Not you, too, Hank. I can see she's got you caught up in her imaginary little world, too. Not that it is any of your business, but I was making love to my wife through most of that night." He gathered up a bunch of files, his uninjured hand trembling. Something slipped out of one of the files and landed on the floor.

Hank reached it before Bruce could and picked it up. It was a photograph.

Hank turned it over and looked at the image. It was a picture of a very young girl, possibly around three years old, sitting on a porch, her knees apart. She was clearly naked underneath a man's plaid shirt, her genitals bare. He winced and handed the photo to Toni.

She looked at the photograph, realizing the shirt was one of Bruce's. Something inside her snapped. "Bruce, if you won't get help with your problems, Hank and I will take this photograph to the police." She handed the offensive photo back to Hank, who slipped it into his pocket.

Bruce went ballistic. "Who the hell do you people think you are, coming in here, stealing my things and threatening me? You sound just like Viv's brother, threatening to tell Viv what happened when Cynthia and I were young. I can phone the police, too, you know, and have you charged with all kinds of things."

By now, Bruce was sputtering, waving his good hand in the air, fist clenched.

Spit was flying from his mouth as he yelled at them. He was coming around his desk toward Toni and Hank when the phone rang. Bruce yanked the phone toward himself.

"What?" he barked into the phone. "Nothing. Everything's just great." He slammed the receiver down.

Toni walked toward Bruce, her manner conciliatory, nonthreatening. "Bruce, I want you to take a bit of time to calm down and then I want you to gather your personal items and leave. Hank and I will wait for you downstairs until you leave. An hour should be sufficient. I'll send Roxie up with some boxes. Pack your client files separately and leave them next to Roxie's desk. I will phone our lawyer and have her begin the dissolution process of our partnership." Without waiting for a reply, she turned and walked out the door, Hank following her.

Chapter 35

Toni called Viv as soon as she could. She and Hank agreed to hold off contacting the police, hoping that Bruce would voluntarily seek help. They had no proof, after all, that anything had happened with the small child in the photo. However, if Bruce still refused help, they would act.

Toni would not be surprised if other women came forward, once word spread, that they, too, had been sexually harassed by her partner. Bruce didn't seem to be bothered by any boundaries, external or internal. Hank suggested that they wait no longer than a few days to take action. Toni agreed. Bruce was a procrastinator, and a sexual predator, but not a killer. Small comfort, she thought to herself.

Viv opened her door when Toni knocked. She looked like she'd been crying. Her eyes were red and puffy and she was blowing her nose as she opened the door to Toni. Toni grabbed her friend in a hug and they stood in the doorway for several minutes, silently. Toni closed the door behind her and brought Viv into the living room to sit on her sofa. She gently asked, "Tell me, Viv. What happened when Bruce came to see you this afternoon?" She took Viv's hands in her own.

"He looked awful, Toni. He was clearly enraged about something. I made him calm down as much as possible, and then he told me. It turns out that our whole life together was a lie. Everything he had told me about his childhood was a fabrication. I felt so sorry for him when he had told me early on about his having to leave his home because his mother cared more about dogs and cats than about him. He was forced to bunk in with his grandparents and sleep on a stair landing in their home for several years, leaving school and working. Finally finding some solace with his first wife. The truth is truly monstrous, and I can't not believe what he told me today. No one would make this up.

"The family had to remove his cousin from their home for several years because Bruce kept trying to molest her. She was sent to live with his mother's best friend when she was about ten. They brought her back home and sent Bruce to his grandparents. They must've thought that sending Bruce away was a safe alternative and would give Cynthia time as a teenager with her aunt, whom she had missed a great deal. As it turned out, Bruce found his way back to their home often and began sexually molesting his cousin, culminating in her rape when he was nineteen. His cousin was fifteen.

"She eloped with her boyfriend and had her first son when she was sixteen. No one knows the truth about her son's father. It could be that her boyfriend fathered him. DNA testing would have solved the question, but that route was not taken.

"Cynthia is dead, and the truth has gone with her.

"I knew that something bad had happened between Cynthia and Bruce when they were younger, but she never said a word, and I also knew there was no point in asking Bruce. He would laugh it off and tell me that I was imagining things.

"What a terrible life Cynthia had... I wish now that she'd had the confidence to confide in me, but I understand why she didn't. No one likes to wreck a marriage, and I'm not sure I would have believed her anyway.

"Apparently, Peter, Cynthia's widowed partner of many years, threatened to tell me about what happened if Bruce didn't.

Bruce probably didn't believe that he, Peter, would do that. Not until today when his world fell apart again. What happened at the office, Toni?" She looked at her friend.

Toni told her, as gently as possible. When Viv heard about the photograph, she stifled a scream with her hand. "My God, no, no, please, please make this not be real." But Toni could tell by her sobs that Viv believed her friend was telling the truth about what had happened today.

She finally turned to Toni, wiping her tears again, asking what could be done. Toni told her what she and Hank had talked about at Bruce's office, the disturbing photograph, the deadline they'd given Bruce and the course of action they would take if he didn't comply.

Viv asked if he could be helped. Toni answered truthfully that she didn't know, that a lot depended upon Bruce's attitude about wanting to be a better person. She explained about how difficult borderline personalities were and how resistant to change most were. She said it might take years of therapy and that there were no guarantees. And, she thought to herself, if women began to come forward with accusations, his goose was doubly cooked, so to speak.

She did not say any of that last possible turn of events. Viv needed her protection and support more than brutal speculations. The road ahead would be full of bumps and potholes, craters even. Right now, Bruce's immediate future was up to him.

Chapter 36

Bruce checked his ticket again as he waited in line at the airport in Toronto. One-way to Vancouver. Great city. Too bad he wouldn't be spending any time there. His last visit to Vancouver was for the Canadian Psychological Association's annual meeting two years before. He had been invited to give a paper about the psychosocial aspects of physically disabled patients in residential treatment homes. What a blast that trip was. He'd hooked up with a perky little blonde psychiatric nurse, Cherie. When not attending the conference, which was most of the three-day event for Bruce and his newly found paramour, they'd amused each other thoroughly at the Comfort Inn. Not only did they break the bed, but at one point they even set off the smoke alarm. Whooee, he smiled in remembrance.

"Sir... how can I help you?" The pretty reservations clerk brought Bruce back to the present. He handed her his paperwork and had his bag checked through to his plane. He walked the lengthy corridors to his departure gate and took a seat. He thought about the days leading up to this moment, shaking his head at the memories.

The idea of him needing therapeutic help was hard to swallow, but the thought of the alternative, possible criminal charges was even less appealing. His erstwhile partner, Toni, and her newly minted boyfriend, Hank, had made it clear that unless he was willing to accept therapeutic help for his "problems", charges would be forthcoming. Hah, Bruce said to himself, I can hold my own with any so-called therapists they can throw at me. I've read the book and not only bought the t-shirt but designed it, too. Let 'em do their best, he thought. There's nothing wrong with me. And, besides, a short stay on beautiful Salt Spring Island is just what the doctor ordered. I can pull the wool over all their eyes and be on my way in a short while.

When his flight reached cruising altitude, he winked at the attractive flight attendant as she handed him his rye on the rocks and a napkin. This is the life, he thought, downing his drink in a few swallows. He closed his eyes for a nap.

His lay-over in Vancouver was brief, and he looked appreciatively at the sunlight bouncing off the harbor, mountains in the background. His floatplane was dismayingly small – about the size of a large SUV, Bruce thought. He settled into his seat, adjusting the headphones that the pilot handed to him. Take off was swift and startling. The sight of the mountains at the edge of the sea did nothing to assuage Bruce's terror at the smallness of the plane or the racket of the engine. He clutched his armrests and began to pray.

"Please, whoever you are, let us land safely as soon as possible, and I promise to do whatever is required of me at the Bella Vista New Beginnings Centre." The knuckles of his hands were white and sweat dripped off his forehead.

The flight was, mercifully, short, and Bruce stumbled as he stepped off the plane onto the dock at Salt Spring Island. He looked up at the gray sky and promised, "Thank you, whoever you are. I swear I'll be good." After thanking the unseen deity, he also told himself to book a return trip on one of the daily ferries at the end of his stay. No more bone-jarring trips over the Strait of Juan de Fuca in a child's toy.

The taxi took him to the center, mid-island, and Bruce

looked appreciatively at the long curving driveway leading up to the administration building, the professional-looking grounds and the modern-looking one-story buildings that dotted the grounds in the distance. Not bad, he thought.

Once registered, he was led by the executive director's assistant to his suite. Not bad at all, he thought, admiring the diminutive waist and spherical rear of the "assistant".

He asked her, in his most charming voice, "Say, what time is your shift over this afternoon?"

Chapter 37

Fred held his baby girl, watching Georgie play with the new set of Duplo Legos that he had given his son. After the terrible events of the last little while, Fred thought he would never tire of spending time with his children. He held Peony close, breathing in the wonderful smell of her wispy baby hair, stroking her soft arm.

Georgie pulled at his dad's leg. "Look, Dadda, Georgie make a house," his face beaming at his accomplishment. Fred admired his son's handiwork, thinking back to the recent events that had finally reunited him and his children.

Larry, his lawyer, had worked miracles in a matter of a few weeks and had not only secured temporary custody of Georgie and Peony for Fred but had also secured a place at Homewood for the treatment of Laura, the children's mother. Larry warned Fred that, given the severity of Laura's alcohol addiction, it looked as though her release date and rehabilitation would be a long time in the future.

"She may relapse at some point, Fred. And if you have any thoughts of picking up where you left off, you need to be aware that the chances of her recovery and long-term sobriety are slim to none. In my experience, determined alcoholics will say or do whatever is expected of them initially in order to regain trust. However, it may be a long time, if ever, before Laura is truly rehabilitated. And, if she is truly rehabilitated, she may be a very different person from the one you married. If I were you, I would be prepared to be single parent for a long time." Fred knew that this was a distinct possibility and one that, given the recent past, he welcomed with all his heart. He'd had his fill of relapses and recriminations.

He didn't hold any grudges against Laura. He knew that her alcoholism was most likely familial in nature, and that it was a disease, not something she had chosen. She had often told Fred about her childhood with her mother and its negative effects on her as she was growing up. One incident in particular stood out in her mind. It had happened when she was about six years old. She had told Fred the story.

"My mom and I walked one evening to a neighbor's house a few blocks away from where we lived. My mother had asked for and been given a drink and had asked for a few more during the course of the evening. It became apparent to our hosts that my mom would not be able to walk home, so they telephoned my dad to come and get us. When we got home, I saw my mom stumble to the stairs, walk up a few of them then fall backwards in a heap on the living room rug. My dad rushed over and helped my mom stand up and then he slowly accompanied her up the stairs to the second-floor bedrooms. A bit later, I was in bed and my dad came and sat beside me and held my hand. Suddenly, my mom rushed into the bedroom and struck me across the face with her arm. My dad pushed my mom out of my bedroom, his words full of anger at my mom."

Nothing was ever said about that night. There were many more incidents of her mother's alcoholism as Laura was growing up. "I would lie awake at night, waiting for my mom to come to bed so that I could creep downstairs and check the ashtrays to make sure that all the cigarettes were out. I was always worried that my mother might leave a lit cigarette downstairs and that our house would be engulfed in flames. I had an escape route worked out if that ever happened. I felt as though I were the mom in my childhood home. I tried to tell her that when I was about twelve. She said that she had no idea what I was talking about."

Laura left home at the age of seventeen to attend university and never went back to live in her parents' house.

When she and Fred met and eventually married, she told Fred that she would never drink in front of her children. However, that vow was broken shortly after Georgie's birth, most likely precipitated by her mother's insistence on spending so much time at Laura and Fred's house to help Laura "take care of the baby". She would ask Laura for a bit of rye to add to her coffee at lunch; that bit of rye became a glass of wine, and that glass became the better part of a whole bottle as the afternoons wore on. And, of course, she insisted that Laura join her in her "refreshment time". Those times eventually extended to the whole of the day, from the minute Laura's mom arrived until she left in the afternoon, always before Fred arrived home.

When Fred came home at the end of a long day of work, Laura was often passed out on the living room couch, their son crying in his crib.

Fred tried to talk to Laura about what was happening and the potential harm to their son. She would become defensive and angry. "Mind your own business, Fred. I'm being the best mother I can be, but I just need a bit of 'help' to get through the days. My mom and I don't drink in front of Georgie, you know," the last said in self-righteous indignation. A few months later, Laura was pregnant again.

She seemed to stop drinking while pregnant with Peony; at least that's what she told Fred. He knew that her mother was still visiting several afternoons a week, but Laura seemed to be fairly sober when he arrived home. He discovered later that vodka and mouthwash were good remedies for hiding what was really going on. Once Peony was born and the sleepless nights returned, so did the mother-in-law and the bottles of wine.

When he came home one evening from a stressful day at a construction site in Acton, he found an empty house and a note on the kitchen table. The note, in Laura's familiar handwriting, told him that she and their children were staying with her parents and that he, Fred, should not try to contact them. In desperation, not knowing what else to do, he had called his sister, Toni.

He now said to Toni, "Looking back, I wonder if I could have done anything differently, anything that might have prevented the disastrous events that followed Laura's pregnancies and the births of our children. I knew that the tie between my wife and her mother was close. Laura didn't seem able to make decisions without her mother's input. Their telephone conversations took up most of the day, beginning when Laura got up in the morning and ending just before she and I went to bed at night. I often thought that Laura and my mother-in-law should live together; it would certainly save on phone bills."

At the beginning of his relationship and marriage to Laura, Fred had thought that his wife's newly formed dependence on her mom might be a good thing. He knew how fractured that relationship was by the time Laura had left for university. They seemed to have patched things up fairly well. Fred was busy building up his construction business and his hours were often very long and stressful. He initially saw his mother-in-law as a godsend, particularly just after Georgie was born.

Laura seemed to have trouble coping with her new role as a mother, and her mom came to their house and assumed a lot of the duties that Laura was having trouble managing while caring for little Georgie and his colic episodes.

As time went on, though, it became apparent to Fred that the relationship between his wife and his mother-in-law was not normal, and that they were caught up in a long-term symbiotic relationship that precluded most other people, including himself.

He told Toni that he often wondered what his role was in his marriage to Laura. "I felt left out, side-lined by her relationship with her mom. I'm ashamed to admit that I was jealous some of the time. My wife put more thought into her relationship with her mom than into our marriage. She was always asking her mom's opinions about things, something that she used to do with me."

Since the recent revelations about Laura and her ongoing addiction problems, Fred was determined that the future with his small, young family would be different and much better. He had found a young nanny, Jen, who seemed to be working out well. "She arrives in the morning before I leave for work, Toni, and stays until I come home at the end of the day, dinner ready, kids bathed, changed for bed and delighted to see their Dadda. And best of all, they seem to adore her.

"Once a week, mom arrives and spends most of the day with her grandchildren so that Jen can do grocery shopping and all the other necessary chores accumulated by a small household. Weekends are all mine with my children, and nothing will disrupt them, ever."

He might not be the world's best dad, he thought, but he knew that his love and determination would see him and his children through whatever else life had in store for them.

Chapter 38

"A medical leave?"

Toni was getting ready for her "special" dinner with James. At the same time, she was thinking about what Hank had told her about his time with James' department head at Athabasca. What type of illness would warrant an indefinite period of time off work? It seemed that whenever she asked James about his health, he changed the subject. She decided that she'd have to be more persistent in her approach with him.

She took her time dressing for the upcoming dinner. A feeling of dread had been gathering inside her all day. So many negative events had happened lately that she had begun to anticipate "turns for the worse", as her mother called them. Whenever her phone rang, she arrived home, or opened her email, she seemed to be blindsided by disaster. Waiting for another "*loosecannon*" shot...

Bruce had announced that he had checked himself into a private treatment facility that he'd found in British Columbia. He had left yesterday for Salt Spring Island. Both Toni and Viv were relieved that he would voluntarily check himself into such a place. Hank said that their deadline approach had probably helped.

Otherwise, Bruce might've been tempted to drag out his period of indecision and exacerbate an already bad situation. Maybe with Bruce's departure, things would return to some sort of normal. She certainly hoped so.

She finished applying her makeup, twisted her freshly washed hair into a French braid and gathered her purse and the bottle of wine she'd bought. "You're in charge, Humph," she said to a sated and somnolent cat. Humphrey opened one eye at the sound of his name then settled more firmly into the rocking chair, his head resting on his tail, his purr loud and steady.

As Toni unlocked her car, she smelled the late-autumn musk of wood smoke and dying leaves. She buttoned the top of her jacket and turned up the heat in her newly restored car. Traffic was light on the darkened streets of Guelph. Lights shone on the black silent river. There were few people on the streets tonight.

Why have I been feeling so apprehensive lately, she wondered. James' behavior the last few days has been especially good. He's been kind to the point of unaccustomed generosity toward her. His offer to cook a special dinner for me tonight is very unusual, I must say. "Maybe too unusual," her ever-vigilant alter ego pointed out. "You know the old saying: 'If it seems too good to be true, it probably is.' Be careful, Antonia."

She pushed the warnings out of her mind as she turned onto Winston Crescent. What a cozy little street, she thought. Most of the houses were miniature Capes, well-kept with meticulous landscaping and suitable outdoor lighting. She found number fifty-eight without a problem. As she turned the wheel to pull into the driveway beside the house, she noticed a dark laneway that seemed to lead behind the houses in the general direction of Metcalf Street. Must be a short-cut to the park, she thought. Maybe James was telling the truth about the dog-walking episode after all. He was certainly offended when I told him I didn't believe his story. Keep an open mind, Antonia.

The light over the side door came on, and James stood on the back stoop, holding the door open for her. She gave him a quick kiss on the cheek as she walked by him.

"Something smells good, James. Don't tell me you learned to cook during your time away?"

"I have lots of hidden talents, my dear. Let me take your coat." He led her into a small kitchen. "Would you join me in a glass of Barolo?" Without waiting for her answer, he took down a balloon glass from a cupboard and poured a large amount of the dark red wine he knew she loved.

As he handed her the glass, he brushed his fingers along the side of her hand.

She felt her stomach clench at his touch. She regarded him carefully as she took a sip of wine. He looked even worse than the last time she saw him. Large pouches of bruised-looking skin hung under his eyes. He was wearing an ascot around his neck, but when he turned his head, she noticed a nasty-looking sore where the ascot's material pulled away from his neck. He looked even thinner than he had a few days before.

Trying not to seem apprehensive about his touch or his appearance, she said, "What a charming little house, James. Are you renting?"

He grimaced slightly and said, "It belonged to a good friend. When he died, he left it to me. Come, and I'll show you the rest of the house." He ushered her into a small living room. She noticed a framed portrait of a handsome young man on a side table.

James led her up the stairs to two small bedrooms and a tiny bath tucked under the eaves. As they entered James' bedroom, Toni saw another framed photograph on the bedside table. The same young man had his arm around a younger, healthier-looking James. They were smiling at each other. "Is that the friend who left you the house, James?"

James gazed down at the photograph with a look of great sadness. "Yes. Tim, in our better days."

The feeling of dread that had been building in her all day had settled into her stomach like a chunk of cement. She knew she had to ask but wasn't sure she wanted to know the answer. "What happened to him, James?"

James led her back downstairs and into the kitchen. "It's a long story, Antonia.

"Let's eat dinner and I will tell you the whole, sad story." He put the finishing touches on the beef stew. Toni sat at the small table in the kitchen's alcove. James brought a small basket of bread to the table and lit the tall tapers that sat in the middle of the table. He sat down and replenished both of their wine glasses then held his up in a toast.

"To new beginnings, Antonia." He stared into her eyes for several seconds then drained the wine in one long swallow. As he put the empty glass onto the table, he began to cough. The coughing went on for a long time, seeming to come from the depths of his chest. When it finally stopped, he wiped his eyes with his linen napkin. "Sorry about that, my dear. Eat up before your stew grows cold." He picked up his fork and gestured for her to do the same. She saw a small trail of blood on the side of his mouth. She tried not to stare.

Toni wasn't sure she could eat anything. Her suspicions had coalesced just like the dread in her stomach. Her head wasn't feeling very clear, either. "Better not drink any more wine, sweetie," said her inner voice.

"Tell me about Tim, James." She picked up her fork and moved some pieces of beef around her plate.

James put his fork down and poured himself some more wine. "I loved him." His eyes sparkled with unshed tears. "When he died, I thought I would die, too. I wasn't that lucky, unfortunately. When I was told he'd left me his house, my only thought was to sell it as quickly as possible. But as time went on, I realized that this might be an ideal opportunity for me to come back to Guelph. I would try to convince you that I had changed and that I needed you in my life again. As much as I loved Tim, I realized that I'd never stopped loving you. You are my soulmate, Antonia." He reached across the table and tried to take her hand.

"James… I'm flattered. I really am." She knew she had to put an end to this but wasn't sure how. "But my life has moved on. What we had years ago wasn't enough to sustain a marriage. I was unhappy, and so were you. Loving each other wasn't enough. We talked all this through years ago." She had to distract him somehow. "Let me make some coffee." Please, let me get out of this terrible situation in one piece, she prayed.

She closed her eyes for a second as she stood up from the table. At the same time, she felt James' hand close around her wrist in a tight grip. She yanked her hand away from him and her wine glass smashed onto the table, splinters of glass flying and red wine dripping onto the floor.

James half-rose from his seat, leaned across the table and gripped her wrist tightly. "Not so fast, bitch," he hissed. His voice was colder than ever.

Her mind recoiled at both the word and the menacing tone. His grip on her wrist tightened. She looked at her hand and barely registered that it was bleeding. Trying to keep the alarm she felt from her voice, she whispered, "What do you want from me, James?" She was shaking, her heart racing.

His eyes had narrowed into slits. "What do I want, my sweet? I'll tell you." His mouth was a slash in his face, his voice full of menace.

"I want you to suffer the way I am suffering, Antonia. I want you to pay, big time. I want you to pay for not standing by me when I was so wrongfully accused. I want you to pay for divorcing me. Most of all, I want you to pay for murdering our child. For murdering James Barrington the Fourth."

As he spat out these last words, he picked up a large shard of glass from the table. The lethal-looking glass glinted in the light of the candles. James' face was suffused with blood, his eyes filled with rage. With one swift stroke, he cut a deep wound in his arm that was holding her wrist. His blood seeped onto the table, mixing with her blood.

"Now, my dear, you, too, will know what it feels like to live with this hellish disease. This disease that kills by inches, that responds to no medication, that will make you a pariah to your family, to your lover. I will make you regret daily that you ever thought you could walk away from me without paying the price.

"Welcome to the world of AIDS, Antonia."

He let go of her arm in order to grab her with his other hand and bring their wounds together in one last gruesome embrace.

Seeing his intent, Toni knocked her body against the table, flinging dishes, cutlery and candles at James. She heard him scream as she raced across the kitchen, flung open the door, ran down the steps and rounded as quickly as she could onto the laneway she'd seen on her way to James' driveway.

She prayed that she had a few seconds' head-start. Her heart was pounding in her ears as she raced down the laneway. She could hear James running behind her, his breathing harsh, rasping. She reached the end of the laneway and ran toward Viv's house on Metcalf. Suddenly, there was a loud thud behind her and the labored breathing stopped.

Toni ran up the steps of Viv's house and pounded on the door. "Viv, Viv," she shouted. "Open up, it's me, Toni. Let me in. Please!" She was sobbing, sweat pouring down her face.

Suddenly, the door opened and Hank grabbed her as she fell into his arms.

Chapter 39

"Are you sure this looks okay, lovey?" Hank stood in front of the cheval mirror in his bedroom, hands on his hips. He twisted his body from side to side, his head swiveling in the opposite direction.

Toni came up behind him and rested her head on his shoulder as he peered at himself in the mirror, a look of skepticism on his face. Their reflection appeared to be Hank with two heads. She giggled at the thought.

"Do I look that bad? I don't have to wear these suspenders." He continued to look worried.

"You look wonderful, Hank. The red-and-green suspenders are a great idea, and the flashing Christmas bow tie is the perfect touch. Giuliana will be very impressed."

"Tell me again how old Giuliana is?"

"She's three and one of your greatest fans. I probably won't be able to wrestle you away from her all evening." This evening would be Hank's first Christmas at the Rossis, or anywhere else for that matter. As a Jew, he was unfamiliar with Christian traditions this time of year and understandably nervous. He turned away from the mirror and held Toni to him while he took something out of his pocket.

He handed her a small box.

He smiled at the look of surprise on her face. "For you, lovey." She opened the box and gasped in delight when she saw the gold heart locket. "Turn it over," he told her. Inscribed on the back: "Antonia and Hank. Always". He lifted the locket from its box, undid the chain's clasp and fixed it around her neck. He turned her toward the mirror. "Perfect," he said.

When she turned back to him, Toni had tears in her eyes. She whispered, "Thank you," before embracing and kissing him with all the love she felt in her heart for him.

The weeks following the tumultuous dinner at James' house had been full of activity, some of which Toni hoped never to repeat. She and Hank had spent hours with police officers going over the events leading up to and including that last evening with James. Because of James' medical condition, Toni would not lay charges against him. He now posed no threat to her or to anyone else.

In addition, when Bruce returned from his therapy in Salt Spring Island, he and Toni had signed the legal papers that dissolved his and Toni's partnership, and he had turned over all his case files to her. Toni had taken over some of Bruce's clients, the ones she felt confident in helping, and handed over others to more appropriate therapists in and around Guelph. After the holidays, she would actively look for another professional to fill the office upstairs in her building.

Viv summed up Bruce's activities post-rehab for Toni one evening over a glass or two of wine. "Bruce is pursuing his dream of moving to the Maritimes, where no one knows him. He told me that his time at the clinic in Salt Spring Island 'cured' all his problems. He's always wanted what he called 'a simple life', living in a small log cabin, growing organic vegetables and married to an orphan. If he can't find an orphan, he'll settle for someone with no family or friends within several hundred miles. He thinks that young women with no family or friends would be submissive and malleable. The last time we spoke by phone, he'd found a nineteen-year-old Asian student and arranged to meet her for dinner. When he arrived at the restaurant, she was there and so were a large group of her relatives.

"He still doesn't get it, Toni. I'm sure he will inflict his lies and problems on someone else for the rest of his life, thinking that his demons will be banished with the 'right' person. He still doesn't understand that you take yourself with you, no matter where you are or who you're with. And that if his problems are unresolved, they will continue to cause chaos with whomever he picks as his next partner."

Viv and Max were going on a trip over the Christmas holidays. They'd splurged and booked a room at The Ritz-Carlton in Montreal for a few days. Viv was now "mom" to Bruce's cat, who was settling in nicely at Viv's house. A mutual friend of Toni and Viv operated a boarding kennel outside of Cambridge, and she had offered to take care of the cat while Viv and Max were away. Viv sounded happy and excited about the trip and very relieved that Bruce was gone from her life.

Toni privately hoped that that was the case, that Bruce was truly "gone". She knew that borderline personalities had a way of bouncing back, like a boomerang or a jobless adult child. She intended to be there for her friend should she ever soften in her attitude toward Bruce.

James was safely ensconced at Hospice Wellington, a long-term care and palliative facility in Guelph. Toni had visited him a few times and looked in again on him just before Christmas. Each time, he looked more ill, thin to the point of emaciation, hooked up to machines and monitors, nursing staff and care-givers in and out of his room frequently. James' spirit, however, was as undiminished as ever. His attitude toward the nursing staff was imperious to the point of abuse, and at her last visit he held a book out to Toni when she came near his bed, his thin arm trembling, his words outraged.

"Look at this, Antonia," his voice hoarse, urgent. Toni took the proffered book and read the title and the name of the author. It was a scholarly treatise on Restoration comedy by an old rival of James. The two had been sniping at each other for decades in various literary journals. "He's stolen some of my best ideas. Just wait until I get out of this damned place. We'll see who's the best, that bastard. I have half a mind to call my lawyer and start a plagiarism lawsuit against him…" His last words were drowned in a coughing fit so severe and prolonged that Toni rang the nurse's bell. By the time help arrived, the front of James' hospital gown was covered with splatters of phlegm and blood.

When James was once more calm and the nursing staff had left, Toni unwrapped a present for James and set it on his bedside table. It was an old photograph of her and James, arms around each other, smiling into the camera. She then pulled something from her carryall and gave it to James. "Giuliana wanted you to have this, James. She knew that I was coming to see you today, and she says her favorite teddy will keep you company until you get better and can come home." James wrapped his arms around the teddy bear, hugging it to his chest, and looked up at Toni tearfully. "Tell her 'thank you,' please."

Toni knew with certainty that she wouldn't be back. A feeling of sadness mixed with relief had washed over her as she leaned over the hospital bed and kissed the top of James' head. She whispered, "Be safe, James, no matter what." She turned at the door to look back at him one last time. His eyes were already closed.

Now, Hank's Land Rover was packed with Christmas presents, most of them from Toni for her large family. The

Christmas Eve Italian fish dinner was part of the Rossi family's traditions. Toni's nieces and nephews would be hysterical with excitement, the adults would be indulging in more alcohol than they should, and Toni's mom and female relatives would be bustling back and forth between the kitchen and the large dining room, putting last-minute touches on platters of food. The smells would be ambrosial.

Toni was amazed at the thoughtfulness of Hank's presents. She was dwarfed by one present that she held on her lap in the car. Somewhere, Hank had found a huge potted azalea for her parents. It was in full bloom, and its white flowers reminded Toni of the white garden her dad had cultivated for years at their old house on Victoria Road. Hank's present to Giuli was perfect: a first edition of Hank's latest children's book, signed by the author, of course.

They parked the car on the street near the Rossis'. Their presents would be retrieved later. Toni spotted Fred's large pickup parked across the street. She smiled to herself, knowing how special this evening would be. When the couple stepped onto the front porch, the door flew open and Giuliana ran into Toni's arms, talking excitedly. "*Zia* Toni, I'm so glad you're here. I need help wrapping a present, and I don't want to ask anyone else."

Toni smoothed hair off the little girl's face, now nestled against her shoulder. "*Buon' Natale, cara.* Say hello again to my friend, Hank."

Hank held out his large hand to Giuli, who solemnly put her tiny one in it. She peered up into Hank's face and said, "Are you my *Zia*'s boyfriend?" Toni could feel her own face flush.

Hank smiled at Giuli and kissed her small hand. "I am, Giuliana, and I have brought you a Christmas present." He handed the book to her.

"Thank you, thank you," Giuli exclaimed. She pushed herself away from Toni, grabbed Hank's hand and tugged him inside the house. "Come open it with me before we have to have dinner." Her task for her aunt was forgotten in her delight with Hank.

Toni heard her father's booming voice, audible in spite of the noisy chaos of the house. "Where you goin', *bella*?" – this was directed at Giuli, who was dragging Hank into the living room. As Toni stepped into the living room, her father grabbed her in a big hug. At the same time, he managed to hold on to Giuli's arm as she pulled at Hank. Her dad released Toni and Giuli and embraced Hank with both arms.

"Welcome to our family, Hank."